Thom...
THE T...

The Daughters, Book Two

C.K. MALLICK

Praise for Valthea: I Read People, Book One of The Daughters:

"Insatiable read. . . . left me anxious to read [C. K. Mallick's] next book. . . . intrigue, mystery, hope, suspense and unexpected eventful twist of events which brought joy and comfort. . . A refreshing display of very talented writing!"
— *Patricia Sofia, short-film producer, production manager*

"Loved this read! Some suspense. Some mystery. A teen-age romance. Some circus acts. Lots of tension . . . twists and complexities. The author definitely has my heart."
— *Shelly Arkon, author of* **Secondhand Shoes**

Filled with intrigue, laced with humor, and sprinkled with romance. . . . a must-read. . . . transported me to Romania through this entrancing story, and I loved every minute of my fictional trip!"
— *Janet R. Rockey, author of* **Fear Less, Pray More**

"The story of Valthea is unique and unlike any YA novel I've ever read. The book offers unusual and exciting settings as a backdrop to driving home important life lessons. . . . Fun read for anyone looking for an out of the box story!"
— *Anna O'Keefe, yoga instructor*

"A beautiful page-turner filled with enigma, wistfulness, and humor."
— *Kobi Page, American teen girl*

"Know a teen (or any girl, for that matter) who wants it all? Love life, career, friends, family? Then this book is for her."
— *Kim Hackett, award-winning author*

Thomasina

THE TWIN

The Daughters, Book Two

C.K. Mallick

Canterbury House Publishing

www. canterburyhousepublishing. com
Sarasota, Florida

Canterbury House Publishing

www. canterburyhousepublishing. com

Copyright © 2019 C.K. Mallick
All rights reserved under International and Pan-American
Copyright Conventions.

Book Design by Tracy Arendt

Library of Congress Cataloging-in-Publication Data

Names: Mallick, C. K., author.
Title: Thomasina : the twin / C.K. Mallick.
Description: First edition. | Sarasota, Florida : Canterbury House
 Publishing, 2019. | Series: The daughters ; book two | Summary: Valthea
 hopes to gain access to her mother's journals in time to understand and
 combat the manipulative attacks of a relative who is using paranormal
 gift against her, just as her dreams are coming true.
Identifiers: LCCN 2018042021 | ISBN 9781945401077 (trade pbk.) | ISBN
 9781945401084 (eBook)
Subjects: | CYAC: Psychic ability--Fiction. | Supernatural--Fiction. |
 Birthparents--Fiction. | Love--Fiction. | Circus--Fiction.
Classification: LCC PZ7.1.M347 Tho 2019 | DDC [Fic]--dc23 LC record
available at https://lccn.loc.gov/2018042021

First Edition: February 2019

Author's Note:
This is a work of fiction. Names characters, places and incidents are either
the product of the author's imagination or are used fictitiously, and any resemblance to actual persons living or dead, business establishments, events,
or locales is entirely coincidental.

Dedication:

Dedicated to daughters, mothers, and grandmothers everywhere

One

"I protest this wedding." A voice shot out from the back of the room.

"Who said that?" I turned. *Aunt Szusanna.*

Her very presence knocked the wind out of me. When had she arrived?

The nicotine-thin redhead stood twenty-feet from the carpet runner laid between the rows of chairs where Sorin and my family and friends sat. She wore a white, brocade couture gown bedazzled with crystals, rhinestones, and pearls. A nine-foot-long, cathedral train trailed behind her. Icicle points topped her tiara. My dove-white, A-line gown paled in comparison.

"Evil snow queen," Sorin grumbled. "What does she want?"

"Everything." It wasn't fair. Years ago. Two sisters. It should've been my aunt who died. Not my mother.

"Don't worry, Val. I won't let her ruin our wedding."

My Grama Alessia's estate set the ideal stage for our formal, Christmas Eve wedding. Strings of gold and white lights illuminated the windows, balcony and the grand staircase. Holly and ivy enwrapped the room's pillar columns. Huge urns displayed massive arrangements of roses, lilies and pine sprays. Candelabras held flaming candles. A fragrant, spruce Christmas tree, dressed in red and gold, towered like a general at the entranceway. Six months ago, after searching my whole life, I discovered my birthparents identity, and that my mother came from the opulent world surrounding me.

Sorin and I, the wedding party, and Romanian Orthodox priest, Father Gheorghe stood on a three-foot-high, ceremonial platform. Minutes ago, in orthodox tradition, Father Gheorghe placed gold metal crowns on Sorin and my head. Sorin wore a tux with a white rose boutonniere. I carried a bouquet of holly, white roses, and evergreen wrapped in a satin ribbon. The swirling waft of baking, cinnamon apple pies, coming from the back kitchen, no longer smelled divine. Aunt Szusanna had that effect.

"Excuse me." Father Gheorghe's voice bellowed through the two-story, open living room. "Did I hear you correctly?"

"Yes, you did." Aunt Szusanna sauntered toward the runner. "I protest this wedding."

I wished our wedding quintet's percussionist crashed his cymbals whenever my aunt opened her mouth. I stood tall. "Aunt Szusanna. There's nothing to protest." She couldn't stop me. I was nineteen and more than ready to take on marriage and my fourth last name since being born.

"Valthea's right." Sorin put his arm around my waist. "Nothing to protest. We're getting married. Today."

I kissed the yellow diamond cross pendant Grama Alessia gave me as an early Christmas gift. She wanted me to have my great-great grandmother's cross before leaving for America. To bless and protect me. That's what the gift note said. She also wrote she'd one tiny thing to tell me before I left Romania. Was it to warn me of my aunt's unpredictability? Something else? I'd learned many family secrets over the past few months. None were tiny.

Aunt Szusanna continued. "Father Gheorghe, I'm concerned for my niece."

"How so?" Father Gheorghe raised his bushy, salt and pepper eyebrows.

"I question Sorin Dobra's intentions."

"That's ridiculous." Sorin faced her. "If anything, we need to question your intention disrupting this wedding and upsetting Valthea."

Dad broke from the groomsmen's lineup. "Father Gheorghe, may I say something?"

Father Gheorghe nodded. "I'm listening."

"Thank you, Father. You know Sorin and Valthea. They did pre-marriage counseling with you. You must know my stepson's intentions are one-hundred percent pure and sincere."

"Psst. Szusanna." Grama Alessia waved to Aunt Szusanna. "Stop this nonsense and come sit down." She gestured for her to join her and Mr. Emil in the front row.

Mr. Emil's dark-red bow tie and pocket square complimented my grandmother's regalia of ruby jewels. A vision of Grama's kindly butler and dear friend of fifty years came to me . . .

Mr. Emil. Two decades ago. Broader shoulders. Darker hair. He opened a boxy, black carry case with a gold fleur de leis on the front. He placed four hardbound journals into the velvet lined case. The embossed initials on each journal read: G. A.

Gisella Adamescu. My mother. My stomach knotted. Where was the case now? Who had it? Did my mom write about her and Dad's love affair? About me? Why was I getting this insight now, of all times? I needed to talk to Mr. Emil. After the ceremony, I'd find a way to bring up my mother and then go from there. Maybe the journals are what Grama Alessia wanted to tell me.

Aunt Szusanna headed toward the wedding platform. What did she hope to gain by protesting my marriage? I sent her the DNA document proving my Adamescu legitimacy back in June. She couldn't touch me or my inheritance.

Father Gheorghe cleared his throat and re-opened his Bible. "Since there's no real reason—"

"Oh, but Father Gheorghe. There is." Aunt Szusanna paused midway on the carpet runner. In the middle of the grand room. In the middle our Christmas wedding. "I oppose this wedding for three reasons."

Father Gheorghe closed his Bible and held it in his arms. "I'm listening."

"Thank you. First, Valthea, my naive, little niece, doesn't know if this young man's marrying her for love or for her recent inheritance. Secondly—"

"Not true." Dad again sprung from the groom's line.

Sorin stopped him. "I got this."

Dad nodded and stepped back.

"Father Gheorghe." My fiancé spoke calmly. "If I may, I'd like to respond to Szusanna Stanislaus's first accusation."

"You may," Father Gheorghe said. "I'm listening."

I wished my extrasensory gift wasn't seeing people's past, but their future. Only three people knew I saw past visions. Sorin, Dad, and my clown friend from Sky Brothers Circus. Aunt Sylvie, the woman who raised me, God rest her soul, also knew. She used to say God gave me extra insight to increase my compassion and decrease judgement. Seeing visions of Aunt Szusanna's past kept me unsympathetic toward her.

"Father Gheorghe, you may ask any of the groomsmen and most of the bridesmaids. I fell in love with Valthea the moment I saw her. I still find her the most beautiful girl in the world. Inside and out."

I flushed in love, despite the witch in our midst.

"All hearsay." Aunt Szusanna flicked her hand in disregard. "The second reason I oppose this marriage, is that these two didn't invite all the Adamescu family members."

"That's not true, Father." My champion held strong. "We invited everyone, including her and her husband, who isn't here."

"I'm not referring to my husband, but a certain, mystery relative." Aunt Szusanna grinned so wide, I thought her face makeup might crackle like a sheet of ice over a lake.

What mystery relative? Only my aunt's husband and our deceased family members weren't present. Wait, was this some sick hint she wanted me dead? Or was there another secret stuffed in the grand Adamescu closet? God, please let me see something, like my aunt talking to the mystery person. No reading came. Too much emotion.

Aunt Szusanna continued toward the platform, her train in tow.

I gripped my bouquet tight. Was my aunt insinuating my mother and Aunt Sylvie were ghosts? I glanced at the staircase balcony and the ceiling. I didn't believe in ghosts, but a chill ran up my spine.

"Father Gheorghe," Aunt Szusanna stopped a few feet from the platform steps. "Here's the third and most important reason these two shouldn't marry. Valthea hasn't told Sorin the whole truth. Or have you, Valthea?"

"I don't know what you're talking about. Why are you doing this?"

"Because it's the right thing to do." She stiffened. "I will tell Sorin for you. Sorin, I'm sorry to inform, but most Adamescu women are unable to conceive. Your bride is most likely barren and cannot give you a child."

Grama Alessia stood. "Stop interfering. Leave Valthea alone. She and Sorin love each other." She wheezed, trying to catch her breath.

"Grama." I handed my bouquet to Miss Katja and hurried down the platform steps, avoiding my aunt. Mr. Emil and I helped Grama Alessia sit.

Sorin squared off in front of Aunt Szusanna. "I love Valthea. I will marry her. And that's that."

"Please, Fa . . . Father Gheorghe." Grama Alessia struggled to speak. "Carry on. With the ceremony."

"Of course, Madam Alessia." Father Gheorghe opened his Bible. "There's nothing illegal or scandalous here. This couple's hearts are sincere. We'll continue."

"Not yet." Apollonia, Sorin's step aunt, and one of the dancers from The Gypsy Royales, stepped out of the bridesmaid line. The thirty-five-year-old resembled a vampiress with her raven-black hair and blood-red lipstick. "You see, Father Gheorghe, here's what's funny." She propped her half-smashed up bridesmaid bouquet on her hip. "What this lady says about barrenness on Valthea's mother's side of the family, is also true on her father's. Sorin knows."

A vision pulled me from the present . . .

Apollonia with her fiancé, Strum. Hours ago. "It's been four years, Strum. When are we going to get married?" He walked away. "There's no hurry. You can't have children."

"That isn't the point. I'm sick of Valthea getting everything she wants."

I'd performed with Apollonia and The Gypsy Royales the summer of my sixteenth birthday. She made the entire summer unpredictable and nerve-racking. Thank goodness I befriended and fell in love with the troupe's fire juggler. Sorin.

"Valthea." She smiled. "You are doubly cursed."

"That's enough, Apollonia." Dad took hold of her arm.

She pulled away. "Not yet, Uncle. What's it going to be, Sorin? Decide. Right now. Do you want to have children and make up for the father who abandoned you when you were a little kid? If so, leave now. Forget Valthea. Go and find yourself a real woman."

"Watch yourself." Sorin shot Apollonia the evil eye. "I know the truth of how I came to be in the Dobra family. What you did, and what ended up happening to my family because of it."

"I don't know what you're talking about." Apollonia posed nonchalant. Her rippled forehead revealed her panic. She retreated to her place in the bridesmaid line.

"Valthea." Grama shooed me from her side. "Go back up there and marry Sorin."

"But—"

"I'll watch out for your grandmother." Mr. Emil winked.

"Okay. Thanks." I held my gown, climbed the two platform steps, and stood next to Sorin.

"Father Gheorghe. You're not listening." Aunt Szusanna spat out her words. Her neck veins swelled. Her eyes turned red. "If you marry Sorin and Valthea, you will regret it. I guarantee you."

"Are you threatening me?" Father Gheorghe bellowed. "A priest?"

"No." She quickly softened. "Heavens no. I am simply reminding you that the guilt of such a mistake, as marrying these two, will haunt you. Follow you. For years to come."

"Excuse me, Father Gheorghe," I said. "May I speak freely?"

He exhaled, as if relieved. "Yes, Valthea. I'm listening."

"Thank you." I faced my aunt. "Aunt Szusanna, in a few moments, Sorin and I will be legally and spiritually married. We've spent time with Father Gheorghe. He knows our values, goals, and love for each other. You can't stop this wedding. You also can't stop me from sharing my inheritance with my husband, dad, or whomever I choose." I glanced at Sorin.

He nodded.

I nodded back. "Aunt Szusanna, you and your selfish, evil ways ruined my mother's life. You ruined the chance for me to know her. Forever. You've ruined a lot of things. But I've decided your terror is over."

"Oh hush. It wasn't my fault Gisella died. Your mother was weak. She'd a heart condition."

"That is only partly true." Grama Alessia stood. Mr. Emil helped her. "Gisella wasn't weak. She was strong in faith and in love. Your jealousy and conniving catapulted a series of events that broke her and broke her heart. This is what caused her death."

Dad's face drained of all color.

I froze.

Sorin stayed close to me.

Gasps and whispers flurried throughout the room.

Grama crumpled into Mr. Emil's arms, sobbing. "She didn't have to die."

It was time. God be with me. "Aunt Szusanna." I stepped forward. "Although I believe what Grama Alessia said is true, I refuse to be held by the chains of anger, resentment, and blame. All that ends now. I gathered my breath. "I choose freedom. Therefore, I forgive you."

Her eyes bugged out in shock.

"You heard correctly. I forgive you. Oh, and Aunt Szusanna, know that the power lies with the one who forgives."

"This is all absurd. I've done nothing wrong. Your paper-thin forgiveness is worthless. I refuse it."

"Doesn't matter if you refuse it or not. A sincere heart, the spoken word of forgiveness, and God's mercy breaks generations of chains. Not only am I free, but my mother is free. My Aunt Sylvie is free. And . . ." I held Sorin's hand. "Our children will be born free."

She scrunched her pronounced nose. "No. This is—"

"Aunt Szusanna, I'll welcome you back into the family when you end your vindictive ways."

"You'll welcome me? Back into my family?" Her cheeks burned bright scarlet. "You and your Gypsy father are nothing but low class, carnival bums. This is my family. She is my mother." She pointed to Grama Alessia and then herself. "And I am the last real Adamescu. I will be the new matriarch." She caught her breath. "You see all this?" She turned in place, pointing to the walls, the ceiling, and the balcony. As she did so, her train followed, bunching up and enwrapping her ankles in fabric. "Soon enough, it'll be my—" She fought to keep her balance, but fell backward, landing in a heap.

The wedding photographer snapped up photos before Alex, her driver helped her sit in a chair.

"Put that camera away before I sue you." Aunt Szusanna sat stiff in her ripped gown, crooked tiara and disheveled updo. "You listen to me, Valthea Luca Sarosi." She flicked back a section of her fallen hair. "I am the sole heir of the Adamescu fortune. You are nothing."

"Szusanna." Grama Alessia held onto Mr. Emil's arm. "Apologize now. Otherwise, you will regret it."

"Really, Mother? What are going to do? Write me out of the will again? You can't. Daddy put me back in years ago. You can't change what he wanted for me."

"Szusanna, you have it all wrong. Your father was the one who took you out of the will. When he realized what he'd done, it sickened him. To make up for his past actions, he wanted everything to go to Gisella, and then Valthea and — "

"You're lying. Daddy favored me. He never wanted me to suffer." Aunt Szusanna smacked the empty seat next to her. "You're making up stories."

"I'm afraid not. After your father died, I was the one who added you back into the will. This means, I can also take you out."

Silence. Scary silence.

"You see, everyone?" Aunt Szusanna spoke to our guests on the both sides of the room. "You see what a sick, dysfunctional family my mother, Gisella, and now Valthea have created? This wedding has cursed itself." She straightened her tiara and stood. "Alex. Get me out of here."

Alex offered his arm and walked her toward the foyer.

Silver, the juggler from Dad's troupe, and good family friend, leapt from the wedding platform and ran toward the front door. He snatched one of the pinecones from a gold basket displayed on the entranceway table next to the coat closet. Silver held the glitter-dusted, prickly pinecone behind his back.

Alex helped Aunt Szusanna with her wrap, and then put on his coat.

"Alex." Aunt Szusanna grunted. "My train."

Alex lifted the hem of her train a few inches from the floor and then shifted, staying behind her as she turned.

"Valthea, try as you may, you'll never be one of us. You'll always be a sniffling orphan, Gypsy tramp, and circus bum. Do yourself a favor. Stay in America. You don't belong here."

"Auntie Szusanna, wait," Silver cheered, approaching her. "A Christmas present from Saint Nicolas." Silver placed the glittery pinecone in her hand.

"Ow!" She dropped it. "How dare you?" She bumped into Alex. "Move, Alex."

"Santa sees all!" Silver said in a singsong voice. He opened the front door with exaggerated flourish.

Wind gushed in, blowing Aunt Szusanna's gown and further messing up her hair. She ducked behind Alex. He led her out.

Silver shut the door and pivoted around. "Bye-bye, now." He scooped up the dropped pinecone and grabbed two more from the basket. He juggled them four rotations. "Ow, ow, ow." He tossed them back into their basket.

Our guests laughed and applauded. I appreciated the tension release.

Silver sprinted to our platform. The groomsmen slapped him high-fives and gave him thumbs-up.

Father Gheorghe wiped his brow with a folded cloth. "Let us, finally, continue with the ceremony. Mr. Dobra." He raised his brow. "The rings?"

"Yes, Father." Dad reached into his tux jacket pocket. "I have them right here." He held out his hand, displaying the twenty-two-karat gold, orthodox cross rings.

Sorin picked the slimmer band from Dad's palm and then tipped it so I could see the engraving inside. It read, Always.

"I love it," I whispered. "Thank you."

He grinned in a way that melted my heart. He slid the band on my right ring-finger, in Eastern Orthodox tradition.

I picked up Sorin's band and held it for him to read the engraving I chose. Forever.

"Thank you, my princess," he whispered.

My heart fluttered. I loved Sorin so much. I was the most blessed girl in the whole — I dropped the ring. It fell and rolled on the flat, ceremonial platform, in what felt like forever and in slow motion.

The silence of held breaths numbed the room.

Dad squatted down and up, quick as a Cossack dancer, and snapped up the ring. "Here you go." He put it in my fingertips. "Don't worry, Val." He forced a smile. Beads of sweat formed on his brow. "It's not a sign of bad luck or anything. Just nerves."

"Thanks, Dad." My hands trembled putting the band on Sorin's finger. "Ooo. Sorry." The ring caught his knuckle skin.

"Val," Sorin whispered. "Take your time. I'm not going anywhere."

Sorin's patience made me feel safe and loved. His ring slid on with ease. Perfect fit.

"God bless you both." Father Gheorghe made the sign of the cross. "May you have a happy and fruitful future. I now pronounce you husband and wife. You may kiss the bride."

Sorin leaned forward and kissed me. For one magical moment, it felt like we left the ground and floated in the air. He kissed me once more and then held my hand. We turned toward our family and friends and took our first steps together toward our wonderful, perfect new life.

Two

I leaned on our beachfront condominium's balcony railing. The cool, salty air from the gulf kissed my cheeks. Morning sun warmed my shoulders. White sand. Teal water. Lido Beach. Sarasota, Florida felt more honeymoon destination than new residence.

"There you are." Sorin stepped out onto the balcony.

"Polo shirt and khaki slacks? You're a Floridian already."

"It's comfortable for school. At least I'm not wearing a Hawaiian shirt." He stepped up behind me and wrapped his arms around my waist. "Quite a backyard we have, isn't it?"

"It's gorgeous. The photos the broker showed us didn't do this place justice."

"Yeah, well, your photos don't do you justice either." He kissed my neck "What are your plans right now?"

"Walk on the beach then stretch."

"Can it wait?" He petted my shoulders. "I'm a half hour ahead of schedule."

I turned around. "In that case, yes."

He pointed to my beach cover-up's shoulder ties. "May I?"

"If you untie them, my cover-up will fall to the floor."

"Pity." Sorin untied each bow and then guided the aqua gauze down my subtle curves to the floor.

I stepped out of the fabric encircling my feet.

Sorin stared at my bikini-clad body as if I were a goddess he'd imagined, but never knew existed. It aroused my excitement.

Sorin kissed me as if a full moon glowed overhead instead of the morning sun. I lost all sense of time, space, and reason. I didn't know or care if I was on our beachfront balcony or his bedroom in Brasov.

He parted my lips with his fingertips and whispered into my mouth. "Come with me." His words barely slid down my throat as he scooped me up and carried me away. He pushed open the door to our bedroom with his foot. He lowered me onto the bed.

My cell phone rang.

Sorin picked it up from the bedside stand and handed it to me. "Look, but don't answer."

I read the caller ID. "Front desk."

"We can't have visitors. We don't know anyone." He pulled off his shirt.

I sat up. "What if it's a package and we need to sign for it? I don't want it to be returned." I recalled the vision I'd seen of my grandmother-in-law, Grandmamma.

The Dobra house in Brasov. Must've been twenty years ago with Grandmamma's face half as wrinkled and mean. She held her scowl, ripping in half several sealed, pink envelopes and then stuffed them into a shoebox filled with other pink envelope halves. She slid the shoebox into her bedroom's bottom dresser drawer and then covered it with a wool shawl.

My stomach cramped. Jesus taught us to love everyone, but this woman challenged me. Two years ago, I'd seen a vision of her taking pink envelopes from her family's mailbox and hiding them. She lied, telling my father he didn't receive any letters from my mom. Were the letters still in Grandmamma's dresser? If so, I had to get them. But how? Silver. He could find the shoebox and then send it to Florida.

"Okay. Answer it quick." He lay back on a stack of pillows. "We need to come back to us."

"This is Valthea Dobra.

"Morning, Mrs. Dobra. This is Aaron. There's a young lady here to see you," he said in his usual smooth bass voice. "She's family."

"Family? Here in the U.S.?"

"Who is it?" Sorin sat up. "Can't be Dad. You're picking him up tomorrow. Who else—"

"Who is it, Aaron?" I put my phone on speaker.

"Her name's Thomasina Stratham. Says she's here from England. Her ID matches." He chuckled. "So does her accent. Want me to bring her up, or do you want to meet her in the lobby?"

"Great." Sorin stormed from the bed to the sliding glass doors. "A scammer."

"Hold one second, Aaron." I took the phone off speaker. "Sorin, honestly."

"What if it's the mystery relative Aunt Szusanna mentioned at the wedding?"

"Don't get your hopes up. Your aunt fabricated all kinds of stories to keep us apart."

"But Grama Alessia hinted at something too. Either way, I want to meet who's downstairs." I put the phone to my ear. "Aaron, will you escort her up, please?"

"Sure thing. Be right there."

"Thank you." I set down my phone and headed to my closet.

"I already don't like this girl for ruining our morning." Sorin put on his shirt. "Aaron shouldn't bring the hustler to our doorstep. Not a safe practice."

I put on a red Sky Brothers Circus t-shirt and a pair of cargo shorts over my swimsuit. "Since when did you become so paranoid?"

"When you became a target. And I'm not paranoid. I'm protective."

We walked through our aqua, black, and white, art-deco meets coastal-style living room. Everything was in its place when we arrived in Florida. Grama Alessia hired an interior decorator and a local home stager to work with us. She wanted to make sure we'd enjoy a Florida honeymoon before I started rehearsing with Cirque du Palm and Sorin started acupuncture school. We did the same for Dad and his condo, a few doors down from ours.

Sorin opened the front door after one knock. "Morning Aaron."

The man in his late sixties had flawless, coffee-colored skin and wore a wristband with a scripture on it. He greeted us with a big smile. "Morning, Mr. Dobra, Mrs. Dobra." He moved to the side. "This young lady—"

"Hello there, Valthea." The girl with jagged cut, black hair, bright green eyes, and six-inch-high boots stepped toward me. "I'm Thomasina. Thomasina Stratham." Her lavender angora sweater and black jeans appeared less outfit than backdrop for her spider necklace of black onyx and diamonds. "Finally. We're together again."

"Mr. and Mrs. Dobra, if your fine here, I'll get back downstairs."

"Of course, Aaron." I nodded. "Thank you."

"My pleasure." He smiled and headed to the elevator.

Sorin stepped between Thomasina and me. "Let's get right to it. Miss Stratham, I'm Sorin Dobra, Valthea's husband. Allow me to guess. You're claiming to be Valthea's long-lost cousin, second cousin, or whatever. You saw an article in a newspaper or online. Read about her recent inheritance and her discovering her family. You saw an opportunity and decided to be an Adamescu."

"Sorin, please." I placed my hand on his shoulder. "Give the girl a chance."

"I will, in a second. So, Miss Stratham—"

"Please," she interrupted. "Call me, Thomasina."

"Fine. Thomasina, if you really did fly from England, you must seriously think your plot worthwhile and us gullible."

"That's enough, Sorin."

"It's all right, Valthea." Thomasina smiled. "It's a bloke thing. He's guarding you. It's quite admirable, actually."

24

"Flattery won't work here. Just tell me how you're suddenly related to my wife."

"Valthea and I aren't suddenly related. We've been related from the time of conception. We're twin sisters."

"What?" I felt like I'd been hit with a stun gun. I grabbed Sorin's arm to keep from crumpling to the floor. He held me straight.

"Is this a joke? Because you and my wife don't look anything alike."

"It's the truth, but we're not identical twins. We're fraternal twins. Fraternal twins often don't look alike."

"Even so, my wife would know by now if she had a sister."

"Not necessarily." She spoke calmly. "I didn't know until I found my adoption papers by accident, six months ago. That's when I found out I'd a sister. Valthea, I don't know your situation or why you weren't told about me. But now that you know, aren't you thrilled?"

I couldn't speak. Was it possible? The girl did favor the Dobra side of the family. Whereas, I favored my mom with my golden brown hair and amber eyes. But why didn't Grama Alessia tell me I had a sister? Was this yet another family secret? Maybe Thomasina was the mystery relative.

"You okay?" Sorin asked.

I nodded, still in a daze.

Sorin pulled me aside. "Val, keep your wits about you. Your grandmother would've told you, you had a sister."

"Excuse me," Thomasina chirped. "I've proof."

We turned.

Thomasina rested her Louis Vuitton briefcase on her leg, lifted her thigh, and then clicked open the case while fighting to balance on one foot.

"Please, Thomasina. Come inside."

"Val," Sorin whispered with clenched teeth. "What are you doing?"

"We don't want her falling on our doorstep, do we?"

"Thank you." Thomasina shut her briefcase. "I'm a bit un-coordinated. Not like you. A major circus star."

"Thanks, but I'm not a major circus star yet, and I'm not overly coordinated in six-inch heels." I showed her into our living room. Morning sunlight shot in from our wall of sliding glass doors.

She sat on one of the aqua and black, geometric-patterned chairs and set her briefcase on her lap.

I pushed aside two aqua-and-white, sequin, shell pillows and sat on the couch.

Sorin sat next to me. "See anything?" he mumbled. "A vision?"

I shook my head.

Thomasina didn't look directly at Sorin, but around him. "Sorin." She snapped open the latches on her briefcase. "Why aren't you happy that your wife has a sister?" She pulled out two manila folders. "Oh, sorry. I forgot to tell you. I'm adept at seeing auras. And Sorin, your colors reveal jealousy and worry."

He huffed. "Sorry, Thomasina. You're wrong. I'm not jeal-ous. I'm protective."

"Auras don't lie." Thomasina closed her briefcase and set it on the floor next to her. She handed me one of the manila en-velopes. "Here you are. Results of my DNA test and the docu-ments from the orphanage."

I wanted to look at the documents but couldn't stop star-ing at Thomasina. "Here Sorin." I passed him the envelope. "You're better with this stuff." Did Thomasina and I look at all similar? We were the same height. She looked Romanian, although more like Apollonia than me. Or were we unrelated? Was Thomasina a hustler?

"Don't worry, Sorin. You're in luck. Valthea's colors tell me she knows how to balance things. She'll allot time for you, even though I'm in her life now."

Anyone could learn to read auras, but did Thomasina also have an intuitive gift? Do psychic gifts run in the family? "Thomasina, you don't have to read auras to know Sorin's upset."

She smiled, as if pleased with herself. "Valthea, I see plenty of medium blue around you. You're fairly balanced, and you keep your emotions in check."

Logical guess. Everyone knows athletes and performers can center and focus no matter the situation or pressure. "Thomasina, how long have you known you were adopted?"

"A year ago, May. I found a folder in a locked cabinet after my mother, the woman who adopted me, died. That June, on our eighteenth birthday, the adoption files opened. I called the agency and discovered my birthplace wasn't London, but New York. My last name wasn't Stratham, but Luca. The woman mailed and emailed me everything. I researched online and found a news story about you. What you shared in that interview, matched every lead I had. I finally managed to put all the pieces together."

"Thomasina, everything you know is available online, including the Adamescu family's wealth." Sorin held my hand and whispered, "Don't get attached. We need to first check her out."

I slipped my hand out of Sorin's. "Thomasina, I'm glad you found me. Sorin, everything's fine."

"What a relief," Thomasina signed. "I've dreamt of this moment since I found out about you. Is it true that our father lives in this same building?"

I felt sick. I'd mentioned about my dad moving to Florida in only one, neighborhood newspaper in Bucharest. Thomasina had done her research. Sorin was right. "I thought you only read one article."

"Are you joshing? I've read and translated every article written about you. I've watched every YouTube video of you in Sky Brothers Circus. Multiple times. I've studied every video of you and our father in The Gypsy Royales. Honestly, Valthea. Don't you want to know everything about me, too?"

"Yes." Emotional vulnerability not only restricted the flow of my seeing people's past, it wrecked my common sense and patience. "Yes, Thomasina. I can't wait to get to know you."

"Hold on, Val. Thomasina, this DNA test is from England. How do I know you didn't—"

"Sorin, are you always so suspicious?" Streams of sunlight splashed through the living room and into Thomasina's eyes, lightening them to a Kryptonite green. "Do you question all good things that come into your wife's life?" She passed Sorin the second envelope. "Have a look. Those are results from an American lab." She winked at me. "Must be hard living with a linear pragmatist when you're a creative artist. But then opposites attract, don't they?"

"Yes. Sorin and I get along great." Something about her made me nervous, but also want to spring from the couch and go with her on a radical adventure.

"This one's from Sarasota Lab North." Sorin gave the papers and envelopes back to Thomasina. "Same lab my hospital uses. Clever girl."

"Clever gets the job done. Sorin, you should appreciate my tenacity. A lackadaisical attitude accomplishes nothing. Valthea, I needed to find you and be accepted by you."

Sorin sat up straight. "At a glance, these indicate that you are family."

I smiled inside. I knew she was my sister.

"But," Sorin continued. "That could mean you're Valthea's second cousin or whatever. You need to do another blood test."

"Sorin, honestly, she's already done two. We'll have someone at a lab interpret it."

"It's okay, Valthea." Thomasina slid the envelopes into her briefcase. "It's not surprising. Sorin doesn't want to share you."

"No, it's not that. Why do spin things around? Plain and simple, we need more proof."

"No need to go on about it." She stood. "I'll get another blood test. Valthea, I'll do ten, if that's what it takes for your husband to feel secure and accept me."

"What a farce. I've got to go to work." Sorin headed toward the foyer. "Let's go, Thomasina, I'll walk you out."

"Sorin, wait. Thomasina, please sit. I'll be right back." I walked with Sorin to the front door. "Sorin, I'd like to spend the day with Thomasina. Get to know her. Even if she's only my second cousin. She traveled all the way from England to find me. I want to give her a chance. Please, I know what rejection feels like."

"Fine. But Val, take her to a blood lab. Call the orphanage in New York. Call your grandmother. Find out if she's who and what your grandmother wanted to tell you. Maybe she's the relative Szusanna mentioned."

"Yes, all that, and have a fun day."

"Babe, I'm sorry. I just don't want you to get hurt."

"I appreciate you trying to protect me, but trust me."

"I trust proof and your visions. See anything yet?"

"No. I can't force them. Besides, only one vision would help. I'd have to see my mother holding two babies at six-months-old or younger."

"Then go to a lab."

Thomasina walked up behind us. "Valthea, after all the secrets we've dealt with up to today, do you think whispering's polite?"

Was this girl sensitive or rude? I couldn't tell. "Thomasina, husbands and wives don't always communicate at full volume."

"Val's right. Listen, Thomasina Stratham, whether you're my wife's sister, cousin, or entirely unrelated, you'd better not hurt her. Because if you do, you'll have to deal with me."

"Sorin. Please." Orphans. We all had our abandonment issues.

Thomasina folded her arms in front of her chest. "Are you daft? I just found my twin sister. I couldn't be happier. Have a nice day at work." She waved. "Cheerio."

He shot her a sideways glance and then took my arm. "Babe, please walk me to the elevator."

I left the door half-open and walked with him. "Sorin, why can't you accept the possibility of—"

"Valthea, stop. Listen to me. I'm doing what you've always encouraged me to do."

"What?"

"Listen to my gut feeling. And you need to do the same. I don't have a good feeling about this girl. Val, remember that framed photo we found at your grandmother's house, six months ago?"

"Of course. It was the first time I saw a picture of my mother. I was a baby. She was holding me."

"That's right. You. One baby. Not two, and not twins."

"Yeah, well, it's hard for young mothers to hold two babies at once. Someone outside the shot probably held baby Thomasina. Sorin, look at the facts. She and I were both born in Syracuse, New York on the same day, and we've the same blood type."

He sighed. "You already believe her, because you want to believe her. I've got to go." He kissed me goodbye. "Just be careful."

I joined Thomasina, who now sat the kitchen bar, facing the gulf.

I pulled two flavored waters from the fridge and two frosted mugs from the freezer. "Thomasina, I've an idea." I set one of each in front of her. "Let's call our grandmother. Grand-mother Alessia."

"Brilliant idea." She poured her drink. "Thank you. I'm de-hydrated from my long journey to find you." She drank for several moments. "When did you want to call Grandmum? Tonight, or tomorrow?"

"Now's a good time."

Three

"Hi, Mr. Emil. This is Valthea."

"Hello, Miss Valthea. You don't have to identify yourself. I know your sweet voice."

"Thank you, Mr. Emil. How are you?"

"Quite well, thank you. I'm afraid your grandmother isn't available to speak at the moment. She's with the accountant in her study. If it's urgent, I can—"

"No, no, don't bother her. She can call me when she's finished."

"Certainly. She shouldn't be long, another ten, twenty minutes."

"Thanks. Uh, Mr. Emil, did you happen to find, you know, what you were looking for?"

"The journals?"

"Yes."

"Took them to the post yesterday. All four. I kept them in their black case and mailed them that way."

"Thank you so much. I can't wait to read them."

"You'll be the first to break each journal's seal and read them. What a precious treasure."

"You're right. As soon as they're delivered, I'll bring them to the bedroom and sit in my cozy chair. I'll read her words as if she were speaking to me. Just me and my mom."

"That's a lovely plan, dear."

We said goodbye, and then I practically skipped into the kitchen. I'd let Thomasina see the journals after I read them through at least twice. "Coffee, Thomasina? Or probably tea?"

"I adore coffee, thank you." She followed me. "When's our grandmum calling us back?"

"Ten, twenty minutes." I poured her a cup of coffee.

She added a ton of vanilla almond milk and then sat at the kitchen bar. "You've an incredible view of the sea."

"Yes. The Gulf of Mexico." I set my coffee and phone on the bar and sat next to her. "We love it. We feel so fortunate." Waves rolled onto the beach shore, covering a million, multi-colored seashells before retreating into the gulf. My mind did the same. It splashed over a million different thoughts before returning to the present.

"Sissy, isn't this lovely? We're together after nineteen years. Goodness. We've oodles to catch up on." Thomasina sipped her coffee.

I couldn't get used to the sissy thing. "Yes, we do."

"I see your aura." She set her cup on the kitchen bar. "You're overwhelmed. Confused. Distracted."

"Logical deduction. I just moved to America and met a sister I didn't know existed. It's natural to have a lot of questions."

"Aw, Sissy. Be happy in the moment. Don't drive yourself mad. All the pieces will come together. They always do. And when they do, you'll be as thrilled as I am."

"That's funny. I'm usually the encouraging, positive one." I warmed my hands on my cup. "Truth is, I am thrilled. I love the idea of having a sister."

"I'm more than an idea." She opened her arms side. "Look at me. I'm fabulous!"

Did she mean that in a fun way, or was she full of herself? I couldn't tell. Either way, she made me laugh. "Yes. You're more than an idea. In fact, you're probably a handful."

"Why, who? Little ole' me?" She posed coy and spoke like a Southern Belle.

A Brit imitating a southern American accent. This girl was fun.

"Val, you want to know what blew my mind, warmed my heart, and made me jump for joy all at once?"

"Yes."

"Receiving my actual birth certificate in the mail from the orphanage. Touching it for the first time and reading my name, yours, and our mum's."

"You have your actual birth certificate?"

"Yes. Do you want to see it?"

"Of course, I do." I followed her into the living room. "I only have a reissued one from when my Aunt Sylvie adopted me."

She giggled. "Sissy, your colors are going bonkers."

I didn't like her reading me. "Obviously. The secrets just keep piling up. Aunt Sylvie should've told me the whole, straight forward truth. Would've been much better."

"I'm sure she did what she thought was best. Although, it wasn't right." Thomasina opened her briefcase. "Secrets are untold truths, and untold truths are lies."

"I don't fully agree."

"Of course, you do. Think about it." She pulled an eight-by-ten, white envelope from her case. "A secret's simply a lie wrapped in box and tied with a big ribbon." She slid a scroll-edged document from the white envelope. "But no worries. Your twin sissy's here to rescue you." She waved her birth certificate and then handed it to me. "Read it aloud."

I trembled. "I can't believe—"

"Go on. Read it."

"Okay, uh, 'Thomasina Alessia Luca. Born June first...Syracuse, New York... one of—' Oh my gosh, it says it right here. It's real. It's all real."

"Of course, it is, Sissy." She hugged me for one second and then snatched the certificate. "But you're reading too slow. I'll read it. 'Thomasina Alessia Luca. Born June first, 1987, at 1:22 p.m. in Syracuse, New York. Father, unknown. Mother, Gisella A. Luca.' Notice you don't see anywhere the name, Adamescu. But hang on. There's more." She gleamed. "I'll read it. 'Fraternal twin sister, Valthea Sylvanna Luca.'" She held it out for me to take.

"I'm happy for you. Better put it back in its envelope for safekeeping."

"Now you understand why I'm ecstatic and couldn't wait to—"

My cell phone rang. The screen lit up. "It's Grama Alessia."

"Perfect timing, Sissy. What a coincidence."

"No coincidence. God's timing. I'll be right back. Hi, Grama. Thanks for calling." I headed to my bedroom.

Thomasina followed me. "Come on, Val, don't be childish. Put her on speaker phone."

I mouthed the word, wait, and then shut and locked my bedroom door. "Grama, I've some pretty amazing news, but also some questions. Today, I met —"

"Dear, can it wait one moment? There's something I must to tell you. I wanted to tell you sooner and in person. But with the wedding, and your moving, I didn't find the right time."

"To tell me that I have a twin sister?"

She gasped. "Who told you?"

"Not my Great Aunt Sylvie, or Aunt Szusanna, or you."

"You're upset. I'm sorry. But then who told you?"

"Thomasina."

"Oh, my heart. You found her. Thank God. Is she well? Where was she?"

"She grew up in England. She found me through circus articles. She's fine. Healthy and all that. But Grama, why didn't anyone tell me?"

"Valthea, we wanted to protect you. We wanted to wait until you were older and able to handle knowing —"

"How old? I'm nineteen. Forget that. Please. Just tell me everything now." I flopped back onto my bed and pulled a pillow under my head. "Everything."

"First of all, I'm so sorry I didn't tell you when you were here in Bucharest. It's just with the wedding and everything. Are you angry with me?"

"No, Grama, I love you. Please, continue."

"My goodness, you're calm like your mother. Well, your sister, she's your fraternal twin."

"I know that much. She's here in Florida."

"She's there? You've met?"

"Yes, and she's excited to speak to you, but first I need to know everything."

"Oh, how wonderful. And, yes, of course. I understand. Going on then. After your grandfather sent your mother to New York, Sylvanna, your Aunt Sylvie planned to adopt you girls. But Thomasina had already been adopted. We were never allowed to know who adopted her and the records were sealed."

"They opened up for Thomasina and me on our eighteenth birthday."

"That's grand. But, goodness. I'm sorry, Valthea." Grama Alessia cried. "I try to do the right thing, but—"

"Grama, don't cry. You did the best you could. I left the bedroom and went into the living room where Thomasina sat looking glum. "Let's go forward. Say hello to your other granddaughter. Hold on."

Thomasina air clapped her hands and then grabbed my cell. "Hi, Grandmum. It's me. Thomasina. Aw, it's okay." She paced, sat, and walked around again.

I half sat on the arm of the couch.

"I can't wait to meet you, too, Grandmum. Oh . . .it's all right. I understand." Thomasina nodded and smiled. "Yes, yes. It's true, Grandmum. I was the one who searched for a year until I found my sister. Your welcome. It was worth everything I gave up. Aw...thank you.... That's sweet. I'm glad my diligence and desire for my family brought us together."

I was thankful for Thomasina's search, but I too searched. Not a year. I searched a lifetime for my parents. Grama knew this. I hoped she remembered as Thomasina claimed credit for completing our family circle. I wasn't the jealous type. But then, I never had a sister.

"All right, Grandmum. I'm going to give the phone to Valthea. She'll put us on speaker phone. Hold on."

I took the phone and pressed the speaker button. "Hi Grama. We're both here now."

Grama Alessia giggled. She cried. She spit out more apologies.

We forgave her again and again.

"Valthea, did you show your sister your birthmark? Thomasina, did you show Val what's physically unique about you?"

Thomasina instantly flushed.

"Here's my birthmark." I lifted my bangs with the edge of my hand.

"The little v on your forehead?"

"Yeah. Hard to see now. It's faded a lot. What's your unique thing?"

"Show her," Grama said.

"Uh," Thomasina mumbled. "I've several special things about me. Which—"

"Your widow's peak, dear. My goodness. You were born with a head of thick, dark hair and an adorable widow's peak."

I waited for her to scoot her bangs side. "Let's see."

Thomasina shrugged. "Sorry, to disappoint you Grama. I hated my widow's peak. Not only the way it looked, but because of that old superstition. I had my hairline altered through electrolysis when I was sixteen."

"Really?"

"Oh well. I thought it adorable. But whatever makes you happy."

"What superstition?"

"The spooky one. It's believed that any man who marries a woman with a widow's peak always die young."

"I never heard that."

"That's because you don't have a widow's peak."

"My heavens, girls. I can't believe you're together in the same room." Grama sniffled. "Thomasina, I beg you. Please forgive me. Try to understand. I had no power or control over your grandfather. But I promise, I'll make it up to you."

"Aw, it isn't necessary, Grandmum. But what'd you have in mind?"

"Thomasina." I pulled the phone from her and walked into the kitchen.

She followed. "I thought Grandmum meant like an airline ticket to visit her. Something like that."

Fibber.

"Thanks, Grama," I said. "But all we need is the truth. No more secrets."

Thomasina pulled on my hand and spoke into the phone. "And Grandmum, all I want is to get to know and love my family."

"You girls are so lovely. It's time you both know the truth. Valthea, I wanted to tell you after your wedding, but—"

"It's okay. This is the perfect time. Go ahead. You're on speaker, so we can both hear you."

"Just tell us the basic facts, Grandmum. Keep it brief. No details."

"Thomasina," I whispered. "I want her to tell us the whole story. Give us all the details."

She whispered, "And make her relive it? Suffer all over again? Don't be selfish."

"The basics are fine, Grama," I mumbled.

"Very well, girls. Your grandfather forbade your mother from marrying any Gypsy. It didn't matter that Cosmo was an exception to the stereotype he believed fit all of them. He ignored the love between your mother and your father and flew your mother to New York to stay with a friend and the friend's wife. When the day came, the couple drove your mother to the hospital. She gave birth without any family around."

"She must've been afraid and heartbroken."

"Oh, Valthea." Grama sniffled. "Not a day goes by without me wanting to change the past."

"But Grandmum, we're here now."

"Yes. You are. Thank goodness. Your grandfather, with the help of his friend in New York, put you two up for adoption within a week."

"I was picked right away by a couple living in London."

"Your mother was distraught. I was too. Thomasina, you were flown with a hired nurse to England. With the adoption file closed, we never were able to check on you. I'm sorry."

Thomasina nodded. "I know you did the best you could."

"Valthea, we rushed you and your mother home immediately after that. We hoped your grandfather would soften after seeing his baby granddaughter. But he didn't. He was a bully and a tyrant. He snatched you from Gisella and took you to a local orphanage. He stripped me of his respected family name—Adamescu—and told the orphanage your name was Valthea Luca."

"How heartless. My poor mom."

"Our poor mum."

"Sorry. Yeah."

"After that, your biological great aunt, Aunt Sylvie took action. She adopted Valthea."

"She gave me her last name, Sarosi."

"At that point, we planned to sneak your mother and you over to your auntie's house as often as possible. But then the unexpected happened. Your mother died."

I put my arm around Thomasina's shoulders as tears rolled down her cheeks. It doesn't matter how long you've known that your mother died. Such a well never dries.

After a moment, Grama continued. "By the time your mother birthed twins in a foreign land, had Thomasina taken from her, and then flew across the Atlantic, her health had plummeted severely."

"Plus, Thomasina, Mom never received the letters Dad wrote her. And she didn't know her letters never made it to Dad."

"Dear, I didn't know anything about that. How did you—"

"Dad and I figured it out. Anyway, thank you for telling us the truth, Grama."

"Yes, Grandmum. Thanks for the info on my shortsighted, bigot grandfather and weak, wimpy mother."

"Our grandfather realized his mistakes before he died, and our mother wasn't weak or wimpy. She was strong and fierce with love. Don't you get it? She died of a broken heart."

"Right. But no more moping now." Thomasina bubbled. "Good news. Not only do I have my birth certificate, I have Valthea's."

"What? How?"

"The agency sent me both when I told them I was flying to America to meet you."

"Let me see it." I wanted to see my mothers and my name on the same document.

"Maybe age is catching up with my mind. I thought your grandfather kept the original birth certificates here, at the house. Such a grizzly bear of a man. He didn't want any orphanage having them. Valthea, before your wedding, I searched everywhere for them."

I whispered to Thomasina, "Why didn't you tell me before?"

She shrugged and smiled like the little girl she was not.

The endless twines of surprises, secrets, and lies braided into a rope noose. I poured a glass of water and sipped it to keep from choking.

"Thanks, Grandmum. We won't keep you any longer. We'll call you later."

"That'd be wonderful. I feel at peace knowing you two are together. Thomasina, welcome to the family."

"Thank you, Grandmum. I love you."

"I love you both, my dears. Bye for now."

"Love you, Grama." I turned the phone off and sat in the chair across from Thomasina. "Why didn't you tell me you had my birth certificate right away?"

"Don't get wonky on me. The certificate was supposed to be the cherry on top. I was supposed to be the cake." She wiped a tear. "Guess I was wrong."

"You're not wrong. You are the cake. I just don't know why you waited to tell me about the certificates. Remember Thomasina, I've had a lot to absorb this morning. Unlike you, I've known I was adopted my whole life. Wanting to see my birth certificate doesn't take away from my joy in meeting you. I'm thrilled you're here."

"That's better." She straightened her spider necklace. "Lucky for you, I'm an understanding person. I accept your apology."

I once read that a high maintenance person is a controlling person. I needed time to get to know my non-twin, twin.

Four

I texted Sorin a photo of Thomasina's birth certificate and then one of mine. I wrote, "I invited Thomasina to stay in Dad's guest room tonight. Ok?"

"Might as well. He'll insist she stay forever if he thinks he has another daughter."

"He does have another daughter."

"Going into class. Keep your guard up. Love you."

"Love you." I deleted Sorin's text. "Thomasina, Sorin's happy for us. I'll call Aaron and ask him to bring up your luggage."

Ten minutes later, Aaron brought a cart packed with Thomasina's five-piece luggage set to Dad's condo. There were no scratches, marks, or old travel tags. Aaron congratulated us in finding each other. He said, 'Nothing's more important than family'. I'd seen a vision from Aaron's past, back when Sorin and I first arrived. Forty years ago, Aaron read in the paper of his twenty-two-year-old son's murder. Aaron never met him.

"Will that be all?" he asked.

"Yes, thank you, Aaron." I tipped him well.

He thanked me and then ambled down the hall, pushing the empty cart.

Seeing visions of people's past offered many life lessons. I saw the visions. I didn't always learn from them.

I helped her with her suitcases. Thomasina insisted on handling the one with her camera equipment. I couldn't wait to see her photo work. Subject says a lot about an artist.

"I'm going to freshen up. Then you can take me out on the town. Give me a few minutes. Okay?"

"Meet you at the elevator in fifteen?"

"Valthea. When I say a few minutes, I mean forty. I need a hot bath."

"Sure. Take your time." I pointed to the guest bathroom. "There's towels, soap, lotion, whatever you need. I'll let you get ready. Meet you in forty."

Back at my condo, I showered and put on a bit of makeup. I dressed in a tan sweater and my favorite distressed blue jeans.

My cell phone rang. "Grama, hi," I answered. "I thought we were going to talk later, but I always love talking to you."

"And I you, dear. Do you have a moment?"

"Yes. Thomasina's at Dad's freshening up."

"Tell me. How are you and your sister getting along? I know you're a sweet girl. Is she? You two aren't fighting, are you?"

"No, Grama. In fact, we've a fun afternoon planned. I'm taking Thomasina to lunch and then shopping."

"Wonderful. But I want to prepare you, dear. You were raised an only child. Siblings bicker. They disagree. Especially fraternal twins. Those tales and rhymes about twins exist for a reason."

"What rhymes?"

"Oh, you must've heard them in grade school. You know, 'Two the same, but not quite. One dark, one light. Always ending in a fight.' Hmm. Or is it, fright. Maybe you've heard, 'One basket, two eggs. One a swan, one a snake' . . . something, something. Goodness, I forget the rest. Anyway, I wanted to check on you. I've heard and seen enough twin drama and tragedy to last a lifetime."

"From who? Where?"

"Fraternal twins go back generations in our family. So, please. Be patient with Thomasina."

"I am. But Grama, when you say tragedy, you can't be referring to my mom and Aunt Szusanna. They weren't fraternal twins." I pulled a pair of socks from my dresser top drawer. "Just sisters. Right?"

"Yes, two years apart."

"Then who—"

"Never mind that for now. It was ages ago. But, I will tell you. One's true colors show up in early childhood. It did with Gisella and Szusanna."

"Colors. You read auras?"

"No, no. The expression, 'one's true colors'. It means one's true nature. For example, your mother sparkled bright yellow. Like morning sunshine."

"What about Aunt Szusanna?"

Silence.

"Grama?"

"Your aunt wasn't sunshine yellow."

"Was she gray?"

"No, dear. Gray feels like nothing or neutral. I love my daughter. But Szusanna's anything but neutral."

"She's a black streak," I mumbled.

"What's that?"

"Nothing."

"I wanted to keep you with your mother in our home. It was impossible. Your Aunt Szusanna was sneaky and extremely jealous. Sylvie and I needed to keep you hidden from your grandfather and his Adamescu name. Which, by the way, my family made our wealth. Not his. But that's another story."

"I want to know everything. At least today, we all have each other."

"Yes. A blessing and a surprise. Tell me, has Thomasina opened to you? Did she have a happy childhood? Were her adoptive parents good to her? I do hope so."

"We haven't got into our pasts yet. I imagine she'll want to tell you everything herself."

"You're right. Oh, and my accountant confirmed your mother's will and its use of the word *daughters*. Gisella's inheritance will be split between you girls. Once you send a copy of her ID's, we'll transfer half the funds to an account in Thomasina's name. He'll email details."

"I'll make sure she has everything she needs until she gets her own money."

"I'll help, too."

"No, Grama. We've enough. Just keep going to the nutritionist and the spa and stay well."

"Thank you for your concern. I'm sorry I called you worried about silly children's rhymes and the past. No doubt, you and Thomasina are both sunshine yellow."

"Thanks. Grama, uh, I know you don't read auras, but what about the rest of the family? An uncle or a distant cousin? Anyone read auras, predict the future, or maybe receive visions of people's past?"

Silence.

"Grama? You still there?"

"I'm here. Just took a sip of water."

I didn't hear her drink anything.

"Valthea. Keep in mind. We're Romanian. We are all intuitive."

"That's what everybody says. But there's got to be—"

"I'm sorry Val. I need to go. Someone's at the door. We'll talk later."

"Isn't Mr. Emil there to get the door?"

"He's on an errand. Bye for now. Love you, dear."

"Love you, Grama. Bye." I stuffed my cell phone in my shoulder bag, slipped on a pair of ankle boots, and headed out the door.

"Perfect timing. How about that?" Thomasina stood in front of Dad's condo, two doors down. She locked his door. "True twins." She slid the spare copy of Dad's condo key into her Louis Vuitton handbag. She wore a maroon, velvet jacket over a lavender-gray shirt and black. miniskirt. She wore thigh-high, black boots and her same spider necklace.

I never thought of wearing fake lashes during the day or when not performing. "You have amazing style."

"I know. Thanks. Is that what you're wearing?"

"Yeah."

"You mean, no." She pulled the condo key from her bag. "Come with me."

"I'm fine." I followed her into the guest bedroom. Her suitcases stood in the corner of the room from the largest to smallest. "Thomasina, I'm comfortable in this."

"You can dress comfortably when you're seventy-five. Not in your twenties." She opened the door to the walk-in closet. The clothes she'd pulled from her suitcase and tossed on the floor earlier, hung color coordinated, from tops to pants.

"I'm impressed."

"Val, you're the new circus star in town. You need to impress Sarasota and your future fans before your first show. Once you're in the ring, you'll blow them away. Thank goodness, I'm here. I arrived just in time."

"I'm a private person out of the ring. I like to stay under the wire."

"It's 'under the radar'. Not wire. Forget that. To be a star, you need to attract and command the radar. You need to present yourself everyday like you're on top of the world. Like that famous American high wire walker and his family. All attention on you." She pulled out a magenta and orange, print wrap dress. "Try this."

"But it's sixty degrees outside."

"You can wear this over it." She lay a long, teal-green, suede jacket on the bed.

"Is it suede? You don't mind me wearing your clothes?"

"It's pseudo suede. I try to dress animal friendly."

"You know Cirque du Palm doesn't have any —"

"Exotic animal acts. I know. Only people acts and well-cared-for horses and rescued dogs. Hurry and change. What size shoe do you wear?"

"Euro, thirty-seven."

"Me too. Here you go." She set a pair of teal, suede boots next to the bed. They looked brand new. She tossed a shoulder bag with silver chain edging on the bed. "That bag's a Stella McCartney. She's my girl. I'll wait in the living room."

A few minutes later, I emerged hip and expensive. "These clothes feel like they've never been worn."

"I care for my frocks. Enjoy them."

"Thanks, Thomasina. I appreciate it. I guess I do need image help."

"You do. Let's go. We're both fabulous now."

We drove to Lido Key and then St. Armand's Circle. We took in the panoramic view from the bridge leading to the key. Watercolor blue sky. Noisy seagulls. Yachts of all sizes floating on the teal bay. I still couldn't believe I lived in such a beautiful city.

An Osprey flew by our windshield, carrying a fish in its talons.

"Did you see the size of that bird's catch?" Thomasina unhooked her seatbelt and leaned forward. "It's a sign, Val."

"I don't know if it's a sign. Ospreys hunt every morning."

"But it scored a huge fish. It's a sign of upcoming prosperity."

"If you say so."

We descended the bridge and continued down John Ringling Boulevard. Exotic palms lined the main street. Hibiscus and jasmine bushes edged the sidewalks. We breezed by shops with awnings, photo-plastered real estate offices, and international restaurants with terrace seating. The people walking the sidewalks wore everything from pastel golf wear to dark business suits to jeans and flip flops paired with a leather jacket. St. Armand's Circle reminded me of Europe, but with a Floridian twist.

"Sarasota's positively luscious." Thomasina lowered her window. "I love London, but the weather there's tough on my health. You're so lucky, Val. You've quite a life, here. Fabulous condo on the water, hunky doctor husband, and the financial freedom to just go out and buy a new wardrobe."

"It's all new to me, too."

"Be cocky, Val. Brag about your luck. I'm not the jealous sister type."

"No reason to be. You were born in the states. You've an inheritance. You've time to take pictures every day and enjoy your new family. All that's left is for you to meet a guy who sweeps you off your feet."

"I hope I meet that guy. I don't see the future. Or the past."

I felt her staring at me. "We're here. The famous St. Armand's Circle, commonly called, The Circle." Distraction's a reluctant psychic's best friend.

"Lovely. Hurry and park. I can't wait to get out and explore."

I wound around the next round-about. "Thomasina, do auras surround cities?"

"I suppose. If I were to guess, I'd say London's a misty-gray and Sarasota's turquoise-blue." She sat forward. "Beachwear shop, French bistro, olive oil store . . . Oh, look how cute. In the center of the round-abouts' are benches, flower-beds, and Greek statues."

"Sarasota's really into their arts. You'll find the name Ringling everywhere. John Ringling was big into—"

"The arts and the circus. Yes, I did a teensy homework." Thomasina flipped down the windshield visor and added more dark-red, lip gloss to her lips. "Too bad you aren't mystical, sensitive, or psychic, Val." She flipped the visor back up. "Or are you?"

I huffed. "That'd be nice."

"Yeah. It would."

"Reading auras must have its advantages." I stopped at the pedestrian-crossing.

"Colors reveal a person's essence in general, but also what they're feeling in the moment. People get nervous when I tell them I read auras. It naturally puts me in a place of power." Her eyes glint with mischief. "It's like they've swallowed a truth serum they can't spit out."

After the fifth person exited the crosswalk, I drove on. "Are there any disadvantages?"

"It's ended many friendships."

"How?"

"My girlfriends always want to know what their boyfriends feel and think. The colors for love are different than the colors for lust. Valthea, most guys exude lust. Unfortunately, girls mistake a guy's lustful attention as love. Wrong. Love takes time for guys. Every book tells you that. All that to say, I know when my girl-friend's guy's lusting after her, but also when he's lusting after me. Happens all the time."

"What do you do?"

"Attempt to shut down my tantalizing charm and Aphrodite appeal." She paused. "I'm kidding. Sort of. There, Val. A spot in front of that confectionary shop. How lovely."

I put on my blinker. "Do you see colors around people instantly, or do you need to concentrate first?" I completed parallel parking after eight steering maneuvers.

"I see colors around people almost all the time, but I ignore them."

"Let's window shop 'til we find a place we want to eat."

"Brilliant."

We passed the confectionary shop, a gourmet deli, and a sculpture gallery/shop.

"By the way, Val, you look fabulous. Thanks to me, and our good genes."

"Thank you. Our Mom was pretty, and our dad's handsome. I can't wait for you to meet him tomorrow."

We walked in silence for a few moments, our gait falling in sync.

"Thomasina, which colors represents lust, and which represents love?"

"My God, Valthea." She threw her head back and laughed. "You're just like everybody else, inquiring about the lamest thing."

"Love's not lame."

"I understand, Valthea. You're worried."

"I'm not worried. I'm just—"

"You want to know how Sorin feels about you, what are his colors. What are yours. Blah, blah, blah. I don't feel like indulging in my superhero powers right now. Can we talk about it later? I just want to relax and have fun in Florida with my sister and new best friend. Don't you want that, too?"

"I just asked a general question. I'm not worried. I already know Sorin loves me and lusts for me."

Thomasina stopped in front of a women's clothing shop.

One of the mannequins in the window wore a turquoise pant suit speckled with seahorses. The other mannequin was dressed in a white, oversized sleeveless dress, accessorized with a huge, coral starfish necklace.

"Onward." Thomasina looped her arm through mine and led us down the sidewalk. "We'll return to that shop on our eighty-fifth birthday."

"Yeah, if it's still there."

She sighed. "What sisters we'll be by then. All our little kinks will be worked out."

I didn't consider her bipolar behavior a kink.

She stopped us in front of a clothing boutique's window displaying two trendy dressed mannequins. "Now, this is more our style. That one's me." She pointed to the mannequin on the left, dressed in a, red minidress with a peekaboo midriff. "And that one's you." The second mannequin wore an olive-green, bell-sleeved top and a brown miniskirt with a fringe belt. "It's all in the colors, Val. You wear may bright, sparkly costumes when performing. But your aura reveals you're an introvert. You're only truly at peace when alone or in nature."

"You're wrong, and auras don't reveal that stuff." Although, she was right. I did like time in nature. "If you think that, why'd you dress me in these clothes?"

"I didn't want you to embarrass me. I also want you to experience what it feels like to be me. In vogue. Free spirited. A real head-turner. Admit it. You think too much. And overthinking isn't sexy. Don't worry, Sissy. I can help you. For instance, if you want to wear a red dress, I'll show you how." Thomasina strutted toward the pedestrian crossing. "Come on. There's an intriguing restaurant across the street."

Her bluntness left me numb. Why did I feel threatened? Was it my athletic competitiveness? Did I need to be faster and better than my own sister? My clairvoyant gift often kept me ahead of people's next move. Seeing the past allowed me to guess the future and know what to do in the present. But with Thomasina, little insight came.

"For God's sake. Stand straight and walk regal. These people walking around us don't know you're a circus star. Act like royalty. Make them at least wonder."

Thomasina played me high and low, fluid as a teeterboard act. Was I in a psychic battle with my own sister?

We walked by a French restaurant with umbrellaed tables set up on the sidewalk. Pink and yellow hibiscus bushes in huge, terra cotta pots cornered their section of the sidewalk. Thomasina plucked three pink ones and kept walking.

"I don't think you're supposed to pick their flowers."

"I'm a tourist. I don't know any better." She smelled them. "No smell. You know, I'd make a great personal shopper. I could find a woman's best wardrobe based on her aura."

"You'd be great at that."

"You're right. I'd be amazing. I love fashion, and people love me." She scrunched her nose. "Problem is, it's hard to like people back when you see right through them."

"You put faith in the colors you see around people?"

"I put my faith in the truth. Unlike my parents. They practically worshipped their psychics, palm readers, and astrologists. It was my dad's idea to book weekly appointments with one of them, on Sundays. My mum went along with it. I hated it. They pulled me out of Sunday School, from the friends I'd made, and my favorite teacher, Miss Lorna B."

"I can't believe they took you out of church to go for psychic readings. When I was little, I loved Sunday school, too. Did the psychics know you saw people's auras?"

"No. But when I told people I saw their colors, I received a lot of attention." She tossed the hibiscus in a sidewalk trashcan. "Funny thing is, anyone can read people."

"There are good guessers and intuitive people. But true clairvoyants maintain a high level of accuracy."

"Practice makes accuracy. Like sharp-shooting, fashion styling, and actresses who cry for the camera. The trick is to observe someone without preconceived notions. For instance, when someone finds out that I'm not a celebrity, they're shocked. I'm colorful, charming, and magnetic. When someone finds out you're a circus entertainer, they're stunned. You look like an uptight, introvert."

"No, I don't."

"Yes, you do."

"I'm not uptight." Thomasina's verbal slaps and passive-aggressive slashes left me bruised and depleted. "How can I be an introvert when I perform solo in front of thousands?" I knew the answer but doubted she did.

"Don't be so defensive. You're a focused athlete. Disciplined. You may perform in front of thousands of people, but you hardly see their faces because of spotlights or whatever. It's completely different than being the life of a party. Like me. Ah," she sighed, as if pleased with herself. "Everyone's different. You aren't passionate like me and Sorin.

That's why Sorin's sexier than you. He says what he feels. He's a stand-up guy. Very protective."

I tried 'turning the other cheek,' but both my cheeks already burned white-hot. What makes someone a bully? I'd figure it out. Families come in many forms.

"Sorry, if I hurt your feelings."

"You didn't. You don't really know who I am."

She smirked. "You fancy yourself a queen, don't you? Even so, I'd keep Sorin close. He's an attractive, young man and you, well, you are who you are."

Was she trying to hurt my feelings?

"Takes all types to make a world. That's why you and I are a proper mix and get on so well. We're completely different. Ooo, let's eat there." She stopped in front of a trendy restaurant with second-story, open-air seating. "We can people-watch, and they can watch us."

I followed her in, queasy from her roller coaster ride of innuendos.

"Wait, better check the menu. I'm on a budget."

"Thomasina, I invited you to lunch and shop. Let's enjoy the day. We've plenty for a delicious meal, our new Florida wardrobes, and still give to others."

"Valthea, you're so sweet. As my sister should be. Thank you."

I crossed in front of her and led us into the restaurant.

She trailed behind me. "What do you mean by, give to others? Tipping?"

"No. Giving back. You know, to those in need."

"Good afternoon, ladies." A sixty-something man, with lacquered hair and facial bronzer, greeted us. "Do you prefer the bar or an upstairs, outdoor table?"

"An upstairs table, please." I spoke before Thomasina had a chance.

He sat us at a table overlooking the circle and handed us menus.

"Thank you."

"You're welcome." The host swished back toward the stairs.

"Great. Another town with no straight men my age." Thomasina opened the book-like menu.

"That's not true. We need to watch what we say. Our words form our beliefs, and beliefs, backed by strong feeling, create the world we attract and live in."

"Are you kidding me?" She continued studying her menu. "You're one of those?"

"I'm not one of anything. I just try to be aware of my choices."

"Told you," she muttered, studying her menu. "You're uptight. I can't even make a comment without you going into a lecture."

"That wasn't a lecture. I was sharing an awareness—"

"You talk like you're superior to me. It's a bloody put-off. You need to stop."

"I didn't mean it that way. I—"

"Val—stop obsessing. I already let it go. I'm over your righteous attitude." She ogled over a tray of food a waitress carried past us. "Those crab cakes looked scrumptious."

Thomasina reminded me of a quick-change artist. The quick-change circus act typically featured a slender female who changed from gown to gown under a tent-like cover held and shaken by her partner. After about three seconds, he lifted it off her, presenting her in a different, breathtaking dress or gown. The six-minute act included about thirteen costume changes. Thomasina needed to stop her quick-change moods and exit her self-centered ring.

"I get it, Val. You feel superior. You want to impart all your wisdom on me in one day, because you're older than me by thirty seconds. Let it go." She brushed her hair off her shoulder and smiled. "Aren't you thankful I searched until I found you?"

Both my parents were good and kind. Who'd Thomasina take after?

"I said, aren't you grateful?"

"I'm grateful." And shaken and stirred.

"I'm sure you would've searched for me. If you thought of it."

"How could I think of it? I didn't know about you. Why are you looking at me like that?"

"Like what?"

"Like you're disgusted with me."

"Poppycock."

"Water?" A waitress stepped up to our table, with a pitcher of ice water.

"Tap water?" Thomasina shuddered. "No. Please bring us two unsweetened, raspberry ice teas. And I'd like a clean knife." She gave her the knife from her place setting. "There's fingerprints on this one."

"Sorry about that. Be right back."

"Val, this place's smashing. Perfect for our first meal together. Sad, we missed a childhood of holidays and an adolescence of talking about boys." She perked up. "But we're the grandest of sisters now."

I now understood the expression, "walking on egg shells." "Thanks for wanting to be family. Your timing's perfect. Tomorrow I've circus orientation, next day I'm off, and then I go right into jam-packed training and rehearsals. My circus performs—"

"End of February through May. I know. It's perfect. I'm a professional photographer. I'll go with you to rehearsals and take photos. They'll love me."

"I think it best if I go to the first few rehearsals alone, check out how things flow. After that, I can ask the director about your taking pictures. Is that your job in England?"

"No. I design and edit websites, documents, etcetera. Not my dream job, but it pays the bills. Photography's my true passion." She held her phone high. "Selfie, say, cheese."

I leaned in and smiled.

She snapped several. We must send this to Grandmum. I can't wait to go visit her on holiday." She held up her phone. "Check it out. You can completely tell that we're sisters."

"You think so?" We didn't look anything alike.

Five

"Val, tell me of your childhood, how you met Sorin, how you got into the circus, you know, everything."

"Okay, then I want to hear about you."

"Best for last." She clinked her glass of tea to mine.

I rattled off cliff notes of my life and showed her pictures of people and places on my cell phone. I said nothing of my clairvoyance. "That's it." I put away my phone. "Your turn."

The waitress brought our main course.

"Looks delish," Thomasina gushed.

"Why don't you enjoy your food. We'll continue talking after lunch. Maybe over ice-coffees."

"You're always thinking, aren't you?"

"Just trying to be thoughtful. I know it's hard to eat and carry on a—"

"I didn't mean thoughtful. I meant thinking. You're always thinking ahead, trying to control the situation." She grasped her knife and fork. "*Bon appetit.*"

Stunned, I lost my appetite. After a few minutes, I picked at my meal with my fork.

We finished. I paid the bill, and we headed out.

"Gourmet coffee shop straight ahead." Thomasina led the way.

We ordered almond-milk, iced cappuccinos to-go.

Thomasina handed me a straw. "I'm excited about our new wardrobes. But most of all, this quality time with you." She hugged me with one arm. "I love you, Valthea. You're the kindest person I know."

I braced for one of her whiplash remarks.

"You love me too, right?"

"We're sisters, aren't we?" Needy Brat.

"Doesn't exactly answer my question." She sucked down at least a third of her ice coffee. "I will say, my visit to America has been quite pleasant so far."

"Visit?" I stopped walking. "You mean, you're here just to say, hi? You've no intention of staying and getting to know me and our Dad?"

"From the bubble of the circus tent to the bubble of a trust fund. Ah, Val. You've no idea what it's like working in the real world."

"That's not true. My auntie kept us on a tight budget. We didn't indulge in—"

"Hush it. You're set for life. Me, I quit my job and spent my entire savings coming here, only to be thrown into the gutter by your husband."

"You've hardly been thrown into the gutter, considering the restaurant we just left and the beach side condo you're staying in. Sorin will calm down. We can figure things out. You've dual citizenship. You can live in the states." We strolled. "What if you had a place to live? What if I covered your expenses for a few weeks, until you received your inheritance? Then would you consider staying?"

"Well . . . yes. We are family. I adore you, and I can't wait to meet my dad."

If she treated me like someone she adored, I wondered what—

"But Val, that's too generous." Her face softened.

Maybe she bullied people out of defense, fear of abandonment, or feeling all alone in the world. Everyone deserves a second chance. "We'll have fun together. Besides, I need you to help make me fashionable and establish my brand."

"It's positively shocking to meet an attractive girl who's also nice and generous."

"Please. I'm making up for all your birthdays I've missed."

"Thank you so much. It'll be great to have my own checking account and know there's plenty of money in it."

What did plenty mean?

"How will I make up for all *your* birthdays? I know," she said, suddenly all light and bubbly. "You need some family photos to put around your new home. Good thing I brought my tripod. I need to be in all the pictures."

"It's a super idea. Now, tell me your life story."

Thomasina used her straw to bat around the ice in her cup. "Your story was riches to semi-rags and now, back to riches. Mine's riches to rags to, I don't know. Limbo."

"You're not in limbo." I put my hand on hers to stop her neurotic ice whacking. "You're safe. Home. All that was our mother's, is also yours."

She flushed. "You know I don't care about the money. I just want us to be close. I don't want to lose you again."

"If that's true, then stay. Stay here with your family."

"I wish our birth mum was here."

"Me, too. But, we have each other."

"I'm thankful for that." She exaggerated her sniffling. "It just hits me sometimes."

"It's still fresh news for both of us. Want to sit?" I pointed to a stone bench, situated within one of the garden-like islands of the area.

We walked on the shell path, encircling the bench, and sat, facing two, life-size Greek statutes.

"My mother told me that my father wanted to adopt a child from Romania. It was the good-hearted thing to do and a terrific way to impress his higher-ups and executive colleagues. My parents contacted the orphanage in New York via the one in Bucharest. They saw several emailed photos, chose me, and secured me with a deposit."

"It's sounds so —"

"Calculated? Yeah. That was my father. I grew up in a two-story home in an upper-middle class, London neighborhood. I'd no siblings and was completely spoiled, which I loved, until my father's business dealings crashed. I was sixteen." She reached down to the shell path, picked up a broken shell, and threw it. "It's tragic. Neither the mum who raised me, or you, or our birth mother, is alive."

A sweet-eyed dove, with a black-feather neckband, cooed, perched on the rain tree next to the male statue titled, Music.

"Thomasina, where's your father?"

"Haven't seen him for years. Rumor is, he's a homeless drunk, But I don't know where. She pointed to the statue. "Let's do a selfie with this guy."

I tossed the last of my ice coffee and posed next to my sister and the statue.

She snapped several with her phone and then showed me. "Lights prettier and brighter in Florida, than it's in England."

"We look a lot more alike in these pictures than we did in our first selfie."

"Fancy that. It's like masters and their dogs. You're now resembling me."

"No, I think it's because we're hanging out and getting comfortable with each other."

"Val, if you already knew some family secrets, and then had a baby, who created more secrets, what would you do? Lie, like Grandmum and Great Aunt Sylvie did? Or tell your kid the truth?"

"Aunt Sylvie didn't really lie. She withheld the truth, waiting for the right—"

"No, Val. She lied."

"I'd appreciate it if you didn't call my auntie a liar. You didn't know her." My throat tightened. "Please be respectful, as I am of your mother who died."

"Terrific. You're oversensitive and complicate things. Just answer my question"

Thomasina pushed all my buttons. Was it instinct, caddy girl aplomb, or a twin thing? "I believe Grama Alessia did the best she could, and Aunt Sylvie made the choices she felt were best. If I held secrets, and then had a baby, I'd ease the information to my child, a little bit at a time until she was old enough to understand and handle the whole truth."

"Valthea, we're nineteen. Are we old enough to handle any secrets? Is there any truth you're withholding from me?"

My face went hot. Did Thomasina read my aura, or was she manipulating me to answer questions she didn't know to ask? "No. Are you withholding secrets from me?"

"Val, please, think before you speak. Try to be logical. Why question you about secrets if I'd some of my own? I don't like secrets. My father didn't consult with my mum when he used our family's savings, the mortgage, my college money, and their retirement accounts, to gamble on a single, high-risk investment that failed miserably. His secretdecision destroyed our family, our lifestyle, and it killed my mother."

"I didn't know. I'm sorry. How did it kill your mother?"

"Hold on, Sissy. I've a question. Give me your honest answer."

"Of course."

She smiled like a mischievous pixie. "Do you think me piggish if I crave hazelnut truffles?"

I felt like a beginner flyer in a family, flying-trapeze act. I'd swing forward and back, afraid to let go, somersault midair, and grab the hands of my sister, the catcher.

"Come on, Val. Across the street. See the sign? European Chocolates." She looped her arm through mine. "I know you want truffles, too. Ah, we're such sisters. When my family was rich, we'd have a decadent dessert every night. Truffles were my favorite."

We crossed the street.

"Did your father ever get another job?"

"My father told my mom all the available jobs in London were beneath his status, and that if he stooped that low, he'd become depressed. Well, guess what? He became depressed anyway. He lay on the sofa, watched the telly and ate junk food. At five o'clock, he'd go to the local pub. Here we are." She opened the shop door.

I stepped forward.

Thomasina cut in front of me. "How divine. I'm getting a dozen. Anything we don't finish, we'll share with Daddy." She pointed. "Ma'am, I'd like three chocolate-raspberry truffles, three pecan pie, and three hazelnut-praline. Val, you pick the last three."

"I'm in training. I don't want—"

"Just pick."

"Okay. Um, pistachio-cardamom."

The lady put them into a lavender paper bag with handles. She plucked one more from her case. "Here's one more, as a gift to you girls. Orange marmalade. Enjoy."

"Thank you so much." I led the way out. "Thomasina, if it's hard to talk about your father, we don't have to."

"No, I want to." She bit into one of the hazelnut-praline truffles. "Life was dandy when my father didn't drink. After he lost everything, he drank a lot. He turned violent. One night, my mum woke me up, and we drove away in the middle of the night."

"Like in the movies."

"No, like in lots of women's realities. My mom got a job as a bookkeeper. She apologized for my father, and for no longer sharing her favorite hobbies, like painting and growing roses. She never complained. She worked hard, held in her feelings, and aged." Thomasina folded and then tucked the truffle bag in her purse. "I miss her."

"I'm sorry for all your family went through." I placed my hand on her shoulder. "Wish I could've been there for you."

She pulled out from under my hand. "But you weren't, were you?"

"Thomasina. How could I have been there? I didn't know you." Was she reliving the pain? "I'm sorry. I'm here for you now."

"Okay." She kicked a shell off the sidewalk and then another one and another one. "We didn't have enough to make ends meet.

My mother took on a second job at night as a customer service operator. I went to school, came home, did my homework and then cooked and cleaned. I hated domestic work. I was more the artsy type. Mum still had her paints, brushes, and a stack of blank canvases. She suggested I paint, even though she was done with it forever."

"Couldn't you paint together?"

"Tsk. Think. Surely you know something besides cart-wheels and flips."

Slap.

She grabbed my forearm. "My mum painted from her heart. Her heart. Do you understand?" The veins in her neck bulged.

I looked at her hand on my arm.

She let go. "My mum told me if she picked up a paintbrush and painted again, it'd open her wounded heart. No way did she dare unearth the graves where she had buried her anger and resentment for my father."

I quickened our pace, hoping increasing her energy output might curb another emotional tizzy. "Your mom shut off part of herself to keep it together and be strong for you. She sounds like she was a phenomenal woman and a loving mother."

"She was the best. My father's greedy nature and inflated ego ended up forcing my mum to give up all her creative out-lets. It was sad. Painting, designing, flower arranging. They made her happy. Buoyant."

I didn't know what to say to that. "I'm sorry."

"Are you?"

Her glare knocked the wind out of me.

She walked away. "Because of my father, I learned to never believe someone's words, only their actions."

"Is that because he—"

"Valthea, didn't you finish high school? I'll talk slower for you."

"You don't need to. I was clarifying—"

"Then listen. My father flattered me and my mom. He bought her flowers and jewelry. He bought me toys and then dresses. It was all for show, like his adopting me. He threw me and my mom crumbs and saved the mass of his earnings for himself and his superstar image." She jabbed her finger into my sternum. "You're like him that way."

I batted her hand away. "I'm not like him. I don't distract or deceive."

"You think you're a superstar. You make a lot of promises. You're so much like my father. I got to be honest, Valthea. That makes me nervous. I've no one in this world except you. Lucky for you, family is everything to me. And I'll love you even if you are a liar."

"Stop right there." I grabbed her shoulders and forced her to look at me. "I don't know what you're like as a person yet, but you are my sister. I love you. I've a plan that might help us get to know each other."

"Okay."

"First, we'll shop for new clothes. Then we'll get you a cell phone with a local number. We'll put you on our family plan."

"Family plan?"

"Yes." I let go of her shoulders. "After that, I'll call my real estate agent and ask her to hunt for a condo for you. In case you decide to stay. On the way home, we'll stop by the post office. We'll make a copy of your birth certificate and then Fed Ex them to Grama's accountant."

"But I don't have it with me."

"Then you can do it tomorrow. Tonight, we'll make dinner and eat together as a family."

"That sounds nice."

There's more. Tomorrow morning, before I leave for Tampa, to get Dad from the airport, I'm stopping by the bank to transfer two-thousand dollars from my account to one in your name. That buys us time and you some security while you decide if you want to live here."

"I'm not asking for you to—"

"I'm not done talking." I took her hands in mine. "Thomasina. It takes time to trust someone when you've been raised on secrets and lies. You need to feel safe. You need to know I love you. You can count on me. Having a little money in the bank will give you a sense of security. Maybe then you can release any defense you're harboring from your past."

"And then we can—"

"Move forward, get to know each other, and have fun. But here's the deal. We're not at battle. We're on the same team. No more verbal abuse. If you do, I'll stop you in your tracks. I don't care where we are. Got it?"

"Got it. Sissy, now that you feel better, can we go shopping?"

Six

"Leave the shower running, babe."

"Okay." I stepped out of the shower and onto our fluffy bathmat.

"Wow. My timing's perfect." Sorin pulled off his wet gym shirt. "And not because the shower's nice and hot."

I smoothed on some ginger lily body cream and wrapped myself in a bath towel.

"Meet you in bed?"

"Perfect," I purred. "Take your time, but not too much time."

"Five minutes." Sorin winked and then stepped into the shower.

I lit a candle in our master bedroom, let go of my towel, and slid under our bed covers. The clean sheets felt fresh and cool next to my warm skin.

Sorin came out of the bathroom with a mop of wet hair and a towel wrapped around his waist. He leaned over and kissed my exposed shoulder, and then locked the bedroom door. We've an hour before Thomasina comes over for dinner. I say, we enjoy it."

"I agree, Handsome."

He joined me in bed.

We kissed with our arms and legs intertwined for several minutes before he pushed the covers back and scooted down toward my feet.

"Just lay back and relax, my beauty."

I did.

Sorin massaged my calves. He massaged my thighs and then my hips.

After several minutes of pleasure, Sorin surfaced and whispered, "My Princess Bride. Let's make a baby."

Two hours later, Thomasina and I rushed through dinner, anxious to call Grama Alessia. We sat at the dinner table, watching Sorin eat, and waiting for him to finish.

Sorin stopped chewing. "You girls do have your similarities. Don't wait for me. Go. Call your grandmother. I'll finish eating in the study. Watch some American football."

"Thanks." Thomasina and I dashed to the living room. I opened my laptop on the coffee table. We positioned ourselves on the couch.

"Hi Grama."

"Hi Grandmum. It's me, Thomasina."

"Hi girls. Oh, Thomasina. Look at you. You're adorable." Grama Alessia giggled. "Look at that dark hair. You certainly favor my sister."

I would've loved to have met her. Val says she was an utterly fabulous woman. I'm sure she would've loved me."

"Absolutely. Sylvie was a loving woman."

I knew it was greedy, but I didn't want Thomasina and Grama Alessia talking about Aunt Sylvie. She was mine. Soon, I'd share the three-million-dollar inheritance from my mother with Thomasina. I was fine with that. But she didn't deserve Aunt Sylvie. Reverence alluded my twin.

The next morning, Sorin pushed open our bedroom door with his shoulder and kicked it closed with his foot. "Hot coffee?" He held two steaming, ceramic mugs. They read, Bride and Groom. A gift from our decorator.

"Absolutely. Thank you." I stretched my arms overhead, kicked off the bed covers, and sat up.

He passed me the bride mug.

I wrapped my hands around the mug and took a sip. "Ahh. Delicious."

"You're delicious."

"Sorin, you know what?"

"I'm a natural barista?"

"That, and…and I'm really glad I came into this marriage a virgin. It makes everything we have so special."

"Is that what made you wait? To make it special?"

"Yes." I smirked. "That and Aunt Sylvie's weekly talks."

"What talks?"

"Since I was eleven, my auntie insisted we discussed things concerning girls and boys, human anatomy, hormones, relationships, intimacy, pregnancy, and STD's."

"Wow."

"Yeah. Wow is right. She started with the light stuff and progressively worked up from there every year. But forget about all that. Sorin, last night, you and I connected on every level. The physical, for sure, but also the emotional and the spiritual. I understand now what all the fuss is about in waiting for the right person. It's amazing."

"I agree. It's hot, but more than hot." He drew open the sheer, floor length drapes and then opened the sliding glass door leading to the balcony. "It is, and I'm the luckiest guy on the planet."

The Gulf of Mexico stretched before us. Sunrise colors flooded our room. Rainbow prisms reflected from a tall, glass vase in the corner. It speckled the walls, our bed, and our bodies with bits of light and color.

"This view makes me think of stories and legends of mermaids and captains, ships at sea, and wild underwater creatures."

"Which are you?" Sorin opened the second sliding glass door. The breeze billowed out the drapes, setting them a sail. "The mermaid or the wild creature?"

"How about I'm queen of the mermaids, and you're that debonair, Neptune guy."

"I like it." He sat next to me on the bed, holding his mug, and posturing himself a king. "To my mermaid queen," he said, in his lowest voice. "To our amazing life, here by the sea."

"To my Neptune, and to our spectacular life." I tapped my cup to his and then sipped my coffee. My heart pounded, and

C.K. Mallick

not from the two sips of caffeine. I set my cup on the nightstand, lay back on our feather pillows, and curved my body into an S-shape. I imagined myself a mermaid sunning on a smooth, oblong rock.

He placed his cup next to mine. "You make a stunning mermaid."

"You're a handsome Neptune. Want to swim together?" I curved my body with grace, but then busted out laughing. "Ugh. I'm so dorky." I covered my face and kicked my feet.

"Dorky, but hot."

"I can't even play a coy mermaid." I pulled the covers from my face and slapped my arms down on either side of body. "I've ruined our game."

Sorin climbed on top of me, pinning my arms. "You've ruined nothing."

"Really?"

"Definitely. I don't need coy when I've a sensual and delicious mermaid next to me."

I didn't know much about auras, but I imagined red and magenta light streaming from Sorin's body toward mine. "You just like the silky lingerie I'm wearing."

"I like you wearing, or not wearing, silky lingerie."

"Want to allow ourselves to be carried away by the sea again, like last night?"

"Definitely." He kissed my neck, my throat, my lips....

"Sorin."

"Yes?"

"Last night I felt, uh, I felt—"

"What?" He pulled me closer. "Did something hurt? I never want to hurt you."

"No, quite the opposite. Last night was thrilling, and believe me, I'm glad I didn't and don't have a mermaid tail. Last night was also surreal. At one point, it felt like, well, like—" I rolled to my side to face him. "Like another soul was present."

"Whoa." He propped himself up on his elbows. "Since when do you see ghosts? Do you see dead people now, too?"

"No, Sorin, not ghosts or dead people."

"Then what?"

"A new soul. Sorin, I believe we conceived last night."

"Really?"

"Yeah."

"I hope you're right." He lay on his side and pulled me close. "But Val, please don't get your hopes up. I don't want you to be disappointed."

"I won't be disappointed. God's timing's perfect. It'll happen."

"You never told me you felt unborn souls waiting to come to earth."

"I don't, but like many women, I'm intuitive when it comes to my own body, and I guess, conception."

"I didn't think I was ready for kids so soon, but the idea of a baby on its way excites me. I hope your right."

"Me, too."

Three-years ago, I saw Sorin as a cute fire-juggler, more Viking than Roma. Now, I viewed him as husband, lover, and friend. In the future? The father of our children. Hopefully.

Seven

"Sorin, Thomasina's coming over for coffee." I cracked open the front door.

"I figured." Sorin sat at the kitchen bar, eating my fresh made the pecan waffles. He scrolled through his emails on his phone.

"I smell coffee." The front door slammed shut.

"Good morning to you, too, Thomasina." Sorin didn't' turn to face her.

"It's not good until I've had at least a cup-and-a-half." Thomasina scuffled into the kitchen, wearing a sweat suit and fluffy bedroom slippers. She shielded her face from the sunlight streaming in from the kitchen windows.

I pulled one of my many circus-themed mugs from the cupboard and set it next to the coffee pot. "Manners are easy. With or without caffeine. Here's everything you need. Make it as creamy or sweet as you like."

"You're a bloomin' cheerleader in the morning." She reached for the coffee pot handle.

I grabbed it and held the pot side. "Excuse me?"

She folded her arms across her chest. "Oh yeah. Our deal."

"Yes. And?"

"Right," she grunted. "Good morning, Valthea. Morning, Sorin."

"Morning," he said over his shoulder.

I set the pot back on the coffee maker and sat next to Sorin at the bar.

"Thank you." She stirred several teaspoons of sugar into her coffee.

"Your welcome."

Sorin leaned toward me. "Amazing. You're not just an aerialist, you're an animal trainer."

Thomasina joined us at the kitchen bar with her coffee. "Nice breakfast, Sissy. Thank you." She forked two waffles, plopped them on her plate and doused them with maple syrup.

"Fuel up. In about three hours, you're going to meet Cosmo."

"Not Cosmo. *Father*. You can say the word, Sorin, because he's my birth father."

"Whatever the case. Be ready. The man has more energy than the three of us put together."

She cut into her soaked waffle. "Val. Rest assured. I'll be perky and Florida-girl fashionable by the time you and Dad return."

"You should be." Sorin finished his coffee. "You'll have three hours."

Thomasina scowled at Sorin. "Sissy, what about your husband's attitude toward *me*?"

"Don't worry, Thomasina. I'm trained." Sorin set his plate in the sink and then fake-smiled. "Have a nice day."

"Sissy, who picked out the décor for the guest bedroom in Dad's condo?"

"He did. Why?"

"Gold walls, angel figurines, photos of our mum. It's a shrine, not a bedroom. He's obsessed."

Sorin grabbed his keys from the foyer table "No, my dad loved her. He's a big hearted, sentimental guy."

Thomasina spun around on her stool. "You're still here?"

"Yeah, I live here. Hey, Thomasina."

"What?"

"When Val returns from the airport, she leaves for her orientation. You'll be alone with my dad for hours. My point is, you better be the real deal. He'll automatically love you if he thinks you're his daughter. You better not hurt him."

"Sorin, Cosmo Dobra is Valthea and my birth father. But we'll continue to share him with you since he took you in after you were abandoned."

Sorin's face reddened by the second.

I shook my head no, reassuring him. I'd said nothing to Thomasina of his origins. But then, how did Thomasina know?

"After breakfast, I'm applying online for jobs."

"Jobs? Where in England?"

"No, Sorin. Sarasota. Val convinced me to stay. Besides, you say my dad's loving and sentimental. I don't need to read his aura to know it'll break his heart if I leave."

"Thomasina, stay and have another cup of coffee with me?"

She shrugged and headed back to the kitchen. "Sure, Sissy."

"I'm out of here." Sorin kissed me goodbye. "Drive safe today, Val. Call me after you and Dad are on the road."

"I will."

I closed the door behind him and joined Thomasina at the kitchen bar.

Thomasina . . . she sat on a single bed in a studio apartment. Next to her perched an unusual camera. She pulled a dozen or so photos from a teal, plastic envelope. She fanned out the photos of people of various ethnicities and ages. Bands of red, yellow, green, blue, pink, and violet shone from the perimeter their head and shoulders. Thomasina opened a huge, hardback book titled, Kirlian Photography and Aura Interpretation. She read from the book and then wrote on the photos with a black marker. She wrote: Angry. Kind. Depressed. Joyful. Drainer.

What was that weird camera? And why'd she need to read a book about—was my sister a fake? "Thomasina, quick question."

"Yes?"

"As an aura-reader, do you find you need to stay mindful, so you don't fall into using your skills for personal gain or manipulation? I've read about psychics who say the temptation's always there because of their—"

"Powers?"

"I was going to say, gifts."

"Val, I'm perfectly in check." Thomasina took her plate to the sink and rinsed it well. "Syrup sticks if you don't rinse it off right away. Wait too long and it's tough to scrub off." She dried her hands. "Enough on that. Announcement. Tonight, you shall have your professional photo-session. I didn't forget you wanted some family photos."

"Thanks, Thomasina. I appreciate it." Was she going to use the weird camera? I didn't care what colors surrounded Thomasina. What I wondered was, if someone lied about one thing, should I assume they'd lie about another?

Dad's flight from New York to Tampa arrived seven minutes ahead of schedule. It had only been twelve days, but we embraced like we hadn't seen each other in years. Once on the interstate, we sped through a basic catchup chat.

"I'm so glad you decided to move to America and work with Cirque du Palm circus."

"You didn't think I'd let you and Sorin move to America without me, did you? Your future children need a grandpapa to babysit them. Ah, what a future we'll have."

"Yes, we will." I took a deep breath. "Uh, Dad. There's one more thing."

He put on his sunglasses. "Blazing sun in January. How absurd and fantastic. Yes, Val? What were you saying?"

"If you're at the beach, and the water's cold, do you prefer taking your time and slowly getting used to it, or jumping in and getting the shock over with?"

He threw his arms in the air. "Jump in."

"That's what I thought you'd say."

"The water here can't be as cold as the Black Sea." He adjusted his seatbelt.

"It's not. It was a rhetorical question."

"For what?"

My heart thumped. "Shoot. I need to stop for gas."

"You're three-quarters of a tank full. I thought we were about an hour from Sarasota."

"Yes, but I'd feel better." I exited the highway. I couldn't tell Dad about Thomasina while driving, not driving safely anyway.

"I'm in no rush. I'm with my daughter."

Dad pumped gas while I went inside the convenience store part of the gas station.

I came out with two waters. "There's a little coffee shop inside. Let's sit and have a coffee and muffin before getting back on the road."

"Coffee sounds good." He brushed his hands on his jeans. "Throw me your keys. I'll move your car."

Once sitting inside, with our coffees and cranberry-nut muffins, I knew I had to tell him. "So, how's Lumi and Dino and the baby?"

"Like I said before, they argue a lot, but they're in love. And they love baby Eleni. She's growing so fast."

"Kids grow fast. When I taught gymnastics to the pre-school kids at Coach Muzsnay's gym, I couldn't believe how they grew from one year to the next. Hey, how's Gabi, I mean, how does Aunt Gabi feel about directing the troupe? And how's little Sofia?"

"Gabi enjoys leading. Little Sofia's already tumbling. I feel like I'm repeating myself. Is there a reason you want to delay taking me to Sarasota?"

"No. Why do you ask?"

"Because I'm your father. I know you. What's up?"

Maybe I wanted to be his only daughter for as long as possible. "Remember when I asked you about getting in a cold ocean?"

"Yeah."

"Well, you like to jump in. So, I'm just going to splash you with some cold water."

"I don't understand."

"There was someone, besides me, that Gisella needed to tell you about." I pulled out a five-by-seven photo of Thomasina from the side pocket of my satchel bag. "Do you want to see a picture of your other daughter?" I handed him the photo. "You and Gisella had fraternal twins."

"Twins?" He held the photo with both hands.

"Yeah, but not the identical kind. Her name's Thomasina. She was adopted by a couple in England. When her mom died, she found the papers with her real last name and then found out about me."

"This is amazing. How fantastic." Dad hopped from his chair, leapt around the table, and sat next to me. "How about that? I've two babies, not just one. We have to meet her."

"I have. And now you will. She's at the condo."

"Here? In Florida?"

"Yes. She researched and found me."

He jumped to his feet and gave me a big hug. "Let's go."

We walked to my car. I started the car as he buckled up.

"Val, I'm sorry. I can't forgive your grandmother or your aunt for what they did to my Gisella. To us. We could've been a family all this time. Why didn't your grandmother tell you about this when you were with her for a month planning the wedding and making arrangements to come to America?"

I headed back to the interstate. "Please don't hate Grama Alessia. The adoption records were closed. She'd no idea where Thomasina was or if she was even alive. Yes, we could've been a family if it wasn't for my grandfather. But then we wouldn't have known Sorin."

"Yes, we would. Gisella and I would've met as we did, had you girls, and then adopted Sorin. We would've lived as a family thereafter. The five of us."

"Yeah, and then Sorin and I would've been step-brother and sister instead of husband and wife."

"I don't want to think about it."

"Well, I thought about it a lot. It's hard. We want every-thing."

"Not everything, Val. Everyone."

I nodded, keeping my eyes on the traffic.

"I want Gisella now more than ever."

"Me, too, but we can't have her. She's in heaven. But Dad, part of her is in Thomasina. We have our family."

"You're right." He held up the photo of Thomasina. "She looks like me."

"Yeah. Kind of."

"She absolutely does. Same dark, thick hair. My green eyes." He tucked the photo under the visor. "Now tell me more. Everything you know."

"I don't know that much. I'm sure Thomasina will want to tell you stuff herself. I know I'm technically older. Thomasina was adopted before Aunt Sylvie could adopt her, like she did me."

"We can restore our family. Put Gisella's soul at ease. What's she like? Ambitious and introspective, like you? Or re-laxed and creative? Or — is she excited to meet me?"

"Very."

"Thomasina coming into my life is a gift from Gisella. My loving her will heal my heartache for Gisella."

That's what he used to say about me.

"How long before we're in Sarasota?"

"Forty minutes to the condo."

"Then let's drive faster."

"I'm going the speed limit. Listen, Dad. Just so you know, Thomasina can be a little, um, moody."

"Do I detect some sibling rivalry?" He gave my shoulder a rub. "Don't be jealous. I'll love you equally. Let's call her." He snapped his fingers. "We've waited long enough. I need to talk to her. Tell her I love her."

"Let's use my car's speakerphone."

"Perfect. Ah, yes. Sometimes life gets better every second, doesn't it?"

"That's because we're in a summer."

"It's January."

"I meant, figuratively. Philosophically."

"I don't know where you got that side of yourself. Not me or Gisella."

I pulled my phone from my satchel. "Meeting a long-lost sister, or daughter, is like entering a *summer* adventure. Dad, you know another standout summer season in my life?"

"Tell me."

"Meeting you and falling in love with your son."

"Thank you, Valthea. But if we have summers, that means we have—"

"Winters. Yeah. My worst? When Auntie Sylvie died."

"Yeah. That was a winter for me, too."

"But while in a winter, as hard as it is, I know God will bring a spring. You know, new beginnings, filled with expectation. Like my preparing for my solo act with Sky Brothers Circus and preparing for my wedding and move to America."

"I like your season philosophy."

"You don't think it's silly?"

"There's nothing silly about you. You're an old soul. Like your mom. Gisella was light but also deep like you. She felt the pain and sadness of others. Sometimes I felt she took it on herself." He shook his head, as if to clear the thought. "She always made a point of speaking kind and encouraging words to her family's housekeepers and gardeners. Or in town, to café waiters and shop workers. Wherever she was, she gave to those who needed it. She saw no one better than anyone else when it came to who deserved kindness and love."

I liked when my dad reminisced about my mom. I learned more about her and saw years of worry leave my dad's face and tension fall from his shoulders. "She was kind of like a healer."

"I never felt comfortable saying that word aloud." He twirled his panther ring once. "But yes. Healer."

I put on my blinker and carefully changed lanes.

Dad rubbed his hands together. "Alright, Val. Time to make your mother happy right now. Let's call your sister."

"I agree." I grabbed my phone from the center console.

"Val, before you dial. Let me assure you. I love you to the ends of the earth. You are my daughter, my first daughter. Nothing can make me love you less, only more. You must never be jealous of Thomasina. She's new on the scene, so I need to get to know her, spend time with her. But you are my first. Always."

"Thanks, Dad." It was exactly what I needed to hear. God blessed me with a kind and generous father. I speed-dialed number four. How would Thomasina act with my dad? Maple-syrup-sweet or silk-web-smooth?

"Val." Thomasina picked up on the third ring. "Plane land? Is Dad safe?"

"Yes, in fact, you're on speaker with—"

"Thomasina. It's me. Your father. I can't wait to see you. I already love you."

"I love you, too, Daddy. I can't wait to meet you."

Daddy? I rummaged through my bag for a peppermint, hoping toget rid of the proverbial bad taste in my mouth.

"Precious Thomasina, I can't wait to hug you. You've a cute accent, and you sound so young."

"Dad, she and I are twins. We're the same age."

"But Val, she feels younger, more vulnerable. You feel older because Sylvie raised you."

"Daddy, how much longer before you're home?"

I quickly answered, "Forty-minutes." I slowed to go through the bridge toll. It was Dad's turn to fall for the sweet side of Thomasina. I loved my sister, but I'd raised the gates. My guard stayed high and alert, and not just for myself.

"Daddy, please talk to me your whole drive home. Promise you won't hang up. I'm so desperate to meet you. You're now my father *and* my mother."

Nausea.

"Aw, Thomasina. You're sweet. You know, when I found out that Valthea was my daughter, I was thrilled. But the knowledge also tore open my heart and re-punctured the wound of my losing your mother."

My heart flopped, and not because we ascended the 174-foot-high, Skyway Bridge.

"I believe meeting and spending time with you will finally heal my heart. Thank you for all the time and effort you put into finding us and then traveling by yourself across the Atlantic to be with us. Or are you married?"

"I'm not married, Daddy. And it was no effort. As soon as I found out I was adopted, I had to find you. We'll heal each other. But we can't leave Valthea out. Valthea, don't worry. We'll heal you, too."

"I don't need healing. I'm happy." Did I really rekindle a stack of pain and sorrow for my dad? Or did he pass the torch to Thomasina to make her feel special since he found out about her second?

Thomasina told Dad her life story, overdoing the poor little girl aspect. He listened and uttered sounds of empathy whenever she paused.

I popped another peppermint in my mouth.

My sister bombarded my dad with a slew of rapid-fire, personal questions. In eleven minutes, Dad told her what he'd confided in me over the two-month period I traveled with The Gypsy Royales.

"Aw, Daddy. Thank you for sharing about your life with me. How many minutes before you'll be here?"

"About thirty." What, she couldn't add now? Yes, I was snippy. I was no longer the only child, but the oldest child. The one who no longer needed special attention.

"Thomasina, we're taking you off speaker for a moment. We'll be right back."

"Really?" I asked.

"Why, Daddy? Let's keep talking."

"Thomasina, Dad said hold on." I jabbed the speaker button off. "What's up?"

Dad peered into the rearview window. "That was a monstrous bridge."

"Sorin said, 154 people jumped from it to their death over the last ten years. Anyway, why'd you want Thomasina off speaker phone?"

"Because, although I'm excited to meet her, I need you to know something."

Another secret?

"I believe everything's in divine order. Valthea, I met you first. You were born first. We bonded before we knew we were bonded by blood." He placed his hand on my shoulder and kept it there. "What we have can never be broken. You will always be my first. Please, remember this as I spend time getting to know your sister."

"I'm sorry that finding out I was your daughter brought you so much pain and sorrow."

"Val, no, let me explain. It's true, finding out you were my daughter reopened many memories, some wonderful, some sad. But the most important thing of all," he said, now using his hands for emphasis. "I found out you existed. You were, and are, living proof of the love Gisella and I shared."

"But you said I tore open—"

"You saved me. Do you understand? You rescued me, not Sorin, not Thomasina. You."

"I didn't know that."

"You're my rock. My first born."

"What about what you said to Thomasina, about healing?"

"I'm a quick study of character, and I can tell you, Thomasina's the one who needs healing."

"So why did you tell her that you needed healing?"

"You tell me, Miss Philosophical."

"I don't know. Maybe, because when we help others heal, we heal ourselves?"

"Bravo. At least, let's hope so."

"We'd better put Thomasina back on speaker before she has a tizzy fit."

"That's why you're my rock. Put her on speaker. I'll tell her of our surprise."

"What surprise?"

"You'll see."

I pressed the speaker button.

"Thomasina. Are you ready to hear the surprise we have for you?"

"Yes, Daddy, but you guys were talking too long. Valthea, you're the rudest sister ever."

"Easy, Thomasina. We told you we'd be back."

"You two argue already? I love it," Dad chuckled.

"What's the surprise, Daddy? Did you bring me something from Romania? Maybe a gold bracelet or a pair of earrings?"

"Thomasina, I just found out about you. How could I have brought you something? Good news is, tonight, I'm going to teach you to cook authentic Romanian dishes."

"*Cooking's* the surprise?" Thomasina grumbled, but then lightened her voice. "Aw, Daddy, that's the best surprise ever. Quality time with you and my culture."

Maple-syrup-sweet.

Eight

I spotted Cirque du Palm's dome shaped arena from two blocks away. I had video-interviewed with Alberto Cerci, the circus's founder and director. Today we'd meet face-to-face. I parked, and then smoothed down my pencil skirt walking toward the office. I opened the glass door.

"Good afternoon," I said to the petite, magenta-haired receptionist. I guessed her to be about sixty-five. "I'm Valthea Sarosi-Dobra. I'm here to—"

"You're early." Her Bulgarian accent made me feel like I was in trouble.

"I don't like to be late."

"Goody two-shoes, eh? Bad luck." She stood, handed me a clipboard and a pen, and then sat back down. "Sign those. We received your emailed contract but need one with your written signature."

I took the clipboard and pen, while reading the name plaque on her desk, sandwiched between two empty candy bowls. "Thank you, Ms. Zanev."

"Call me Milly. It's circus," she said in a flat tone. "Everyone's on a first name basis here. We're family." She pulled a bag of chocolate-covered raisins from her desk drawer and filled both candy bowls. "Candy?"

"No, thank you."

She scooped a fistful and poured them into her mouth.

"Milly, are you by any chance related to *The Zanev Riders*?"

"But of course." She chewed quickly and stood, extending one arm, as if presenting herself. "They are my family."

"Really? They're amazing. I've seen videos. They're one of the best trick-riding acts in the circus world."

"Not one of the best. They *are* the best. My husband and I taught our children, and they taught theirs. The Zanev's outperform any of other riding acts. My grandchildren represent the tenth generation in our circus family."

"You must be proud."

"We Zanev's are legacy. Our acts weren't choreographed in circus schools but developed through generations of parents teaching their children. Circus families live and breathe their art, their act, and the world of circus. We press on past the risks and demands, day after day. The Zanev's are the best in the world because of our skill and our heritage."

"Artists from circus families often do standout."

"Not often. Always. We're in a class of our own, and real circus people never age. Look at me. I'm sixty-six and fit as a tiger."

"Uh, yes. You look fantastic for a *fifty-six-year-old*." I told the truth, but also hoped to ease her defensiveness.

"Are you done signing, yet?"

"Almost. Milly, you must be happy for the kids who come and study here. Even though they weren't born into a circus family, they want to learn and maybe have a circus career. We've a lot of circus schools in Europe."

"Valthea, I'm from Europe. I've performed in, or been involved with, circuses four-times as long as you've been alive. There's nothing you can tell me I don't already know."

"Right." I stood and handed her the pen and clipboard.

She unclipped the contract from the clipboard. "This way." She stepped out from behind her desk and led me down the hall.

At least, Alberto Cerci, born into a circus family, didn't mind my circus school background. On one of our phone interviews, he told me he's thrilled every year with the number of kids who sign up for circus art classes. If they don't become performers, they'll be lifelong circus fans and supporters.

Milly guided me around the corner. "This little building-turned-offices, was built in 1996, replacing the one built in 1957."

"What about the arena?"

"That was built in 1958." She stood to one side of an office with its door open. "Alberto, here's your new girl."

"Thank you, Milly."

"You're welcome." She walked away without another acknowledgment of me.

"Good morning, Mr. Cerci." I took two steps into his office.

"Valthea." Alberto Cerci walked around his desk and gave me a warm, Italian hug. "It's great to finally meet you in person. And please, call me, Alberto. Have a seat. May I offer you coffee? Water? Soda?"

"Nothing, thank you, Alberto."

"Nonsense. Try one of these." He pulled a bottle of something from the mini-fridge in the corner. "Florida's humid. Got to hydrate."

"Thank you."

"Glass?"

"No, thank you, this is good."

"I've my whole staff drinking it. Coconut water with antioxidants. Got to take care of your family." He held up his half-full bottle of the same drink. "And you're part of that family now. Salute."

I held mine up. "Salute." I took a sip. It tasted like a Hawaiian cocktail. "Thank you, sir. I'm excited to be part of it. I've always believed that's what it's all about. Family."

"We definitely have that in common." Alberto sat back in his black leather chair and told me of his two sons in college, his daughter who just gave birth to his first grandchild, and of his wife, whom he lost to cancer two years ago.

I offered my condolences and then answered his questions about Sorin, our trip to America, and our adjustment. He passed me a sheet of paper with a list with the names and numbers of professional services he recommended. It covered everything from a good housekeeper to the best attorney in Sarasota. I also told him of Thomasina, and he congratulated me, tapping his water bottle to mine. I sipped some and then twisted in my chair to face the circus posters lining each of his office walls.

"Nice, aren't they?" He pushed off his desk, rolling his chair to the side, and then pointed to the three posters behind him. "These date from the nineteen-thirties to the fifties. The most recent ones are in the reception room, and our hallways are lined with posters from the sixties to the nineties."

"I've always loved circus posters, especially vintage ones."

"Audiences are seduced by our circus poster. They buy a ticket expecting dazzle and thrills. They pray the adrenaline rush spills into their everyday life. So, you see, we've a job to do." He pointed to the vintage poster on the wall to the right of us. "This is one of the best."

Yellow, black, red and green, the framed poster featured a female trapeze artist, flying toward a handsome male catcher. The block-letter headline read, The Flying Mejeras.

"Unfortunately, with this one, there's not only a circus story, and a love story, but a tragedy." He rolled his chair back to the center of his desk. "But let us focus on the future, shall we, Valthea? One with a happy ending. Come." Alberto stood. "Let me show you around."

Alberto talked about Sarasota while following me out of his office.

My thoughts stayed with the artists in the poster. What happened to them? Did they die in each other's arms, or rather, out of each other's arms? A chill shot up my spine. Circus artists are well-trained, thorough with safety precautions, and don't live in a state of fear of the fluke. We know accidents happen. A stuck canon, a caught or snapped pulley-wire, a slip of the hand, and a million other possibilities. I stopped thinking about the poster.

"Ahead, to the left, we've our wardrobe building and dressing rooms." Alberto guided me down a short hall, out a back door, and into a small back yard, of sorts.

I followed him down a path of stepping stones, spotted with fuchsia petals. A grandmother oak stretched wide on our left, and fuchsia Bougainvillea wove around and through a short wood fence.

"Over there's the concession area."

"It's quaint."

"Yes. Perfect for our youth program. The tent where you perform is grand. You'll see. Just like in Germany or Ireland or Italy. Colorful and fun, much like Cirque du Soleil."

We continued toward the arena. Alberto shared a brief history of Palm Circus Academy and named some of its most notable graduates. "Our students not only perform several times a year in school shows, but also at fundraisers and our community outreach programs."

"I like that the school's staff is involved in those kinds of things. I can't wait to help and participate in everything."

"Thank you, Valthea. Our staff and the children's parents all participate. Watch your step."

I stepped over the break in the stone path to the narrow sidewalk. "I guess, donations make a difference for not-for-profit organizations."

"More than a difference. They're everything. For instance, your generous donation allowed us to buy additional seating for our circus tent. I can't thank you enough for that."

"Your welcome. After signing with you and Cirque du Palm via email, my grandmother, my husband, and I, did some research. We liked your outreach programs. Inspired, we put some of our funds together. We received your letter of donation acknowledgment soon after. We were glad to help."

"It's greatly appreciated." Alberto stopped. "We hold charity events and provide outreach programs, but our shows are the heart of our organization. That's where we reach the greatest number of people. The ring master explains to the audience, before each show, how their ticket purchase not only buys them a superb night of entertainment but helps the community and outreach programs."

"That's wonderful."

"Yes, but by morning, audiences only remember their family's fun, the spectacular costumes, and all the thrills." He shrugged, palms up, classic, New York Italian-style. "Eh, what are you going to do?"

"I guess, audiences are psyched for a visual and visceral experience more than an educational one."

"I suppose. In a world filled with greed, destruction, and hatred, people just need to laugh at a clown tripping over his floppy shoes, fall in love with a pretty, talented aerialist, or feel their pulse race while watching wire-walkers form an eight-person pyramid. By the way," Alberto said, winking. "This season, you're that pretty and talented girl in the air."

"Thank you. I hope to inspire people. I'm living proof dreams can become realities."

"You'll definitely add intrigue to our line-up. Tell me." Alberto held his arms out wide. "What do you think of this place and of our philosophy?"

"I love it, and I agree with you. My dad says it best, 'entertainment's good for the soul'."

"I like that. I look forward to meeting your father in person tomorrow. We hired him to teach only part-time and help with lights, but it may turn into a full-time job."

"Either way, he's excited. He's a passionate man."

"Yes, that was obvious from my first video chat with him. You're just as passionate, Valthea, but a quieter version. No one makes it in this business without it. I expect an artists' passion to ripple out into the audience."

"That's what I hope to do." I loved Alberto's thinking. "I feel a responsibility to make that happen every performance."

"Good girl." Alberto quickened his pace. "I knew you were that way. Do you know what happens when like-minds align and then take action?"

"Magic?"

"Exactly."

In Sunday school, they told us that when more than one person prayed together, power resulted. My child-like mind took that concept and applied it to other areas of my life. I knew when circus artists, choreographers, and directors, worked together, magic resulted.

"Valthea, I feel like you've a good mind for imagination. Feel free to brainstorm some theme ideas for our youth circus school's spring performance. I'm considering everyone's presentations in two weeks. I know it's not much time, but our coaches start putting routines together as Cirque du Palm's season begins."

My knees almost buckled. Had Alberto read my mind? Was he psychic, or was God confirming my next desired path? "I'd love to. My future goal is to choreograph or assist direct."

"Wonderful. Not all performers want to be involved on the creative end. I wasn't sure if you did."

Not psychic.

"In that case, Valthea, I look forward to seeing what you come up with. Just don't let it distract you from your training, your act, or your new husband." Alberto winked, pulling his ringing cell phone from the clip on his belt. "Yeah, Milly?"

A man in black pants and black polo shirt walked by, carrying a wrench. "Afternoon."

"Hi."

Alberto clipped his phone back on his belt buckle. "Valthea, one of my board members needs to discuss something. Here comes Milly. She'll take you to the arena. You can stay if you like and watch the rehearsal going on. I'll see you day after tomorrow."

"Thank you, Alberto, and thank you for meeting me today. I'm honored to be part of your circus."

"Our circus, Valthea. It takes all of us. We're more than happy you've joined us."

"Romeo and his crew are in the arena right now. You're going to love him." Alberto walked toward the office, as Milly approached.

"Yes, sir. Thank you again." My stomach flipped with excitement thinking of meeting the world famous, Romeo Bach.

Milly walked in front of me. "This way."

I followed her on the sidewalk, past where part of the concrete lifted. Apparently, the grandmother oak needed to stretch its roots. A light breeze blew. A fluttering of yellow flowers, from a blossoming tree overhead, danced around us for several seconds before bowing to the ground.

I'd never seen a photo of Romeo Bach without his spiked-out, signature blue-black hair, smoky-eyes, or rock star inspired costume. In the ring, Romeo Bach's character combined the appeal of Edward Scissorhands and The Xmen's, Wolverine with a punch of humor and heart. His acts included him performing multiple circus acts, in the air, or on the ground. Everyone from kids to grandparents loved him. But who was Romeo Bach in real life? Disciplined athlete? Splashy showman? Or dreamy daredevil?

"Romeo Bach isn't just the most famous daredevil-clown in the world. He's a twelfth-generation circus performer."

"I read that. He's remarkable."

"That's right, and he's remarkable partially because of his family legacy."

Milly's subtle digs didn't bother me, but her leisure walking style did. I wanted to sprint the fifty-yards to the arena. I'd watched a bunch of Romeo Bach's most recent YouTube videos over the last week. I needed to meet him.

Milly stopped in front of one of the arena's side doors.

I opened the door for her, and then followed her into the partially lit arena. Stadium seats encircled two sides of three separate, but close together, performance rings. Thick gymnastic mats covered much of the cement floor in the middle ring. Dozens of ropes, lines, cables, aerial webs, and silks hung and draped from the ceiling. I couldn't help but sigh with satisfaction. Circus tent or circus arena. I was home.

Milly's shoe heels clicked on the bare cement walkway encircling the ring. "We seat 246. Forty rows of stadium seats, ten columns high. Classes are held here, as well as some rehearsing for contracted professionals. Something's always going on." She embellished certain points of her narration with the graceful movements of her hands. Grandmother-aged Milly's veins, sunspots, and wrinkles seemed to fade away when her ballet and acrobatic training, and decades of performing, took over. One day, besides memories, photos, and costumes, that'd be the only thing left of my career. Elegant hands.

"Milly, this place's incredible. Thanks for showing me around." A vision of Milly's past came to mind. I pushed it away, wanting to focus and prepare to meet the great Romeo Bach.

"The arena wasn't as incredible before one of our board members, C. C. Cornelius funded the air conditioning system for this huge place. You're lucky. You get to work with A/C and Romeo Bach."

"I feel super blessed."

"You sound like him."

"Him, who?"

"This way." She led me along the three-foot high, cement edging, looping the ring. "In Romeo's closing act, he'll run, jump, and perform various tricks on that." She pointed to the fifty-foot-tall, rotating steel apparatus known as the Wheel of Destiny. "Valthea, this is a special show. Romeo Bach and the Wheel of Destiny draw huge crowds all around the world. Alberto wisely hired Romeo this year to specifically guarantee success for Cirque du Palm's twenty-year-anniversary show."

"That makes sense."

"Alberto knows what he's doing."

We stopped center, about fifteen-feet from where five men worked together rigging some contraption. Which guy was Romeo? The skinny guy with a ponytail? The buff, bald man? Whoa, did Romeo Bach wear a wig to perform? What about the other guy in all black? No, his rounded upper back gave him away as a video-game addict. The other two guys appeared to be crew guys. One wore a tool-belt. Circus artists always double-checked their equipment, props, and rigging. Sometimes they set it up themselves, but would the world-famous, Romeo Bach?

"Excuse me." Milly waved. "Romeo, there's someone here to meet you."

One of the men, about five-foot-eight, turned around. "Morning, Milly." The handsome, late-twenties man beamed with energy. "Who's this?"

Romeo Bach wasn't *Romeo Bach*. The clean-cut athlete jogged toward us, His piercing blue-eyes, pale skin, and combed-to-the-side, blue-black hair, reminded me of *Superman*, or better, Clark Kent.

"Good afternoon, Romeo. This is Valthea. She's from Bucharest."

Romeo's warmth and even-keel manner contrasted his gladiator-cut physique. "Welcome, Valthea. I'm Romeo Bach." He held out his hand.

I shook it, unable to speak.

"I speak five languages but, I'm sorry, not Romanian."

"No problem, I speak English. I'm thrilled to meet you. Uh, you still have my hand."

"Sorry." He let go. "Hey, ever see my shtick illusion? I shake hands with of an audience member and their hand disappears."

"Yeah, I saw it on YouTube. It totally stumped me. Hysterical."

"Thanks. I did my homework on you, too. Your grace reminds me of my grandmothers. She was an aerialist, a ballerina in the sky. Nowadays, the air's filled with spunky boys and girls and their supersonic tricks. I'm young, but I'm sentimental. Personally, I like superior skill showcased in either gags, magic, danger, or beauty."

Romeo Bach. Dreamy daredevil. No disappointment. Not that I was crushing on him, but rather, honored to—

"That's why Alberto picked you."

"Excuse me, Romeo," Milly said. "Remember, she's the new girl, schooled, not raised in a circus family. She has to prove herself."

"If Alberto chose her, she's already proven herself. Valthea, I've seen your videos. You're a skilled artist. A dangerous beauty."

"Thank you." I prayed I hadn't flushed.

Romeo Bach . . . a sturdy six-year-old. He turned flips on the full-size trampoline positioned in the center of his family's acre-wide backyard. The afternoon sky darkened with rain clouds. Little Romeo climbed down from the trampoline and ran to a long, knotted rope hanging from a massive oak tree. He swung on it until lightning flashed nearby. He ran full speed, laughing all the way, into the house, and into his bedroom. He grabbed the trumpet laying on his bed and played a Mariachi-type of tune with confident gusto. The trumpet was one of a dozen instruments displayed or setting in his room.

Daredevil and prodigy. It's true. Who we are at six, is who we are as adults.

"Very nice meeting you, Valthea."

"Fantastic meeting you." Romeo didn't flirt or undress me with his eyes, like most guys. His respecting me, made me respect him more, not just as a circus star, but as a man. "Sorry to take you away from your practice."

"You're not. I'm happy to meet you. Since I don't believe in coincidences, and we're working in the same show, there must be a reason. We've things to learn from each other. Heal. Share . . ."

I'd no idea Romeo Bach was so deep. "I don't believe in coincidences either." Wait, was he stating a belief or inferring something?

"It's a coincidence," Milly grumbled. "Alberto booked this show like he does every show. Logical and varied."

"Hey, Rome." One of the crew guys yelled. "Bungee's ready."

"Thanks. Be right there." Romeo took my hand and kissed it. "Until next time, Valthea. Back to work for me."

"Nice meeting you. I'm honored to be in a show with you."

"Likewise, and Valthea," he said, over his shoulder, running back into the ring. "Nothing's a coincidence."

Nine

"Ready for tea and biscuits, British-style?" Thomasina held a tray with a complete tea-setting.

"Sounds intriguing." I pushed away from the dinner table. "I'll clear the dishes."

"Leave them. I'll do them later. Come. Let's go into the living room." Dad led the way. "Tonight's special. We're all together for the first time."

"It's also special because Daddy helped me bake these shortbread biscuits. Or *cookies*, as you call them."

"Dad helped?" Sorin laughed. "I'm afraid."

"Very funny." Dad put Sorin in a headlock. "You weren't afraid to eat a double serving of *samale* or *mamliga*."

Sorin maneuvered out the lock and then draped an arm over Dad's shoulder. "Don't fret, girls. We're just playing around."

Thomasina huffed. "Just like little boys."

"It happens often." I stepped down two-steps into the condo's most unique feature—a sunken living room.

Thomasina set the tea tray on Dad's bronze-edged coffee table, positioned in the center of his masculine, eight-piece, leather sectional couch.

I moved the coffee table book on sport cars to the side. "Thomasina, you and Dad could've relaxed today. You didn't have to cook and bake."

"But I'm glad you did." Sorin slapped Dad on the back. "Val and I haven't taken the time to make Romanian food since coming to Florida. It was outstanding. Thank you both."

"We had fun." Thomasina sat next to Dad.

She appeared sunshine-yellow. Was it her or her yellow-and-white, daisy-print sundress? Maybe having family back in her life made her feel safe, and therefore happy. Or maybe it was my depositing two-thousand dollars into her account.

"Cooking's easy when there's two people." Dad winked at Thomasina.

"Yes, it is."

I placed cloth napkins on the table. "Dad." I glanced at the living room. "I love the choices you made with the decorator for this room, the whole condo."

"Yeah, Daddy. Like this room, you're manly, yet opulent."

"Yeah, that's him." Sorin nudged Dad. "Manly and opulent."

The rich décor reminded me of an East-Europe in days-gone-by. It combined dark woods, leather, and bronze with garnet, gold, and amethyst. The garnet-red wall displayed two rows of family photos on either side of a huge portrait painting of my mom. A gift from Grama Alessia.

I sat next to Sorin.

"Here you are." Thomasina handed us each a cup. "Normally, we'd have these biscuits at teatime. But there's no teatime in America." She passed everyone a teaspoon and then centered the tea-tray, complete with sugar, cream, and lemon slices.

"After you each fix your tea, I'd like to make a toast."

"Ha!" Dad chuckled. "You take after me."

"How?"

Sorin took a biscuit from the tray. "Warning. My dad loves toasting to everyone and everything, and he gets emotional doing so."

Sorin spoke less and less against Thomasina. Thank God. I took a bite of my biscuit. Everyone chit-chatted away and fixed their tea. My mind drifted. I imagined my mother sitting with us on the couch, and the five of us sitting close, sharing funny stories of the past, like normal families do on holidays or Sunday afternoons. How fun it'd be. Although I never knew her, I missed her.

"Val?"

I couldn't wait for my mother's journals to arrive. Learn more of her, discover her inner thoughts and musings.

"Val?"

"What?"

"What do you think?"

"About what, Dad?"

"About us cooking Romanian at least once a week."

"Daddy's brilliant. Earlier, he made a good point. By learning to cook and enjoy the food of my heritage, with its flavors and spices, I'll bond deeper with the culture I missed out on."

Dad ran to his I-pod, setting on a back table. "Food's only one way to connect. Son, how do I work this thing? We need to introduce Thomasina to Romani music, and I need it for my announcement."

"What announcement?" Sorin hopped over the back of the couch. "Don't mess with it, Dad." He scooted in front of him. "I got it."

I took one of the velvet pillows from the end of the couch and relaxed back, tucking my legs in cozy. Watching Sorin, Dad, and Thomasina work together to make it a special night flooded me with gratitude. Grama Alessia was right. Give it time, and it'll come together like a delicious stew.

"Here's the newest Romani pop group." Sorin blasted the music. It bounced with a polka beat. He hooked arms with Dad and they circled around each other, dancing with full energy.

"Here we go, Sis." I stood from my cozy spot and linked arms with her. We danced, twirled, and cheered.

"See, Daddy," Thomasina yelled over the music. "You are ready."

"Ready for what?"

Dad waved a handkerchief overhead. "Yahoo. To meet women."

"What?" I stopped dancing.

Dad ran over to the I-pod and lowered the volume. "That's my announcement." He clapped once, as an exclamation point. "Tomorrow, Thomasina's making me a profile-file-thing and signing me up on several online dating sites."

"That's awesome, Dad." Sorin gave him a quick bear hug. "Wow. Finally. Valthea and I've been asking you to do that for years."

"Why now, Dad?" I asked. "Is it because we're in America?"

"Partially. I am in a different country. It does gives me a wider perspective. Plus, Thomasina made me realize, I'm still young and have a lot of love to give."

One by one, without words, we took our prior place on the couch.

Dad gulped his tea. "Val, you know, my wanting a sweetheart in my life, doesn't erase my precious past with your mother. I will always love and treasure her. There's no one like your first love. But I want a companion to share my life with, like you and Sorin have each other. Are you comfortable with that?"

A burst of several flashes of Dad praying variations of the same prayer.

Why this vision now? If I knew he prayed every day for a wife, I could've done something to help. "Yeah, Dad. I'm more than comfortable with your decision. I'm elated. Like Sorin said, we've encouraged you for years to date."

"I guess Daddy wanted and needed to hear it from me. Don't feel bad. People are always drawn to me and want my advice."

"I believe someone wanted to make a toast tonight." Dad jutted over to the wet bar in the corner of the living room. "Hey, kids, how about some sambuca over crushed ice?"

"Sounds delicious." Thomasina carried the tea tray to the kitchen.

"Just a sip for me," I said. "I'm in training."

"Half a glass, for me." Sorin pulled me to lounge back with him on the couch.

Thomasina returned and joined Dad at the wet bar. "How can I help?"

"Carry those two. I'll carry these."

Dad handed us the chilled rock glasses of the milky white drink.

"First, to Valthea." Thomasina held up her glass. "Never have I seen such a ring of pink."

Dad clinked his glass to the rest of ours and drank. "Ah, Valthea's promise ring. Yes, fantastic, isn't it? Sorin picked it out himself."

I held up and pointed to the pink sapphire promise ring Sorin gave me two Christmases ago. "He thinks you're talking about this."

"Daddy." She giggled. "Sorry, I didn't clarify. Not jewelry. Auras. I see auras."

Dad's face lit up. "Really?"

"Uh, oh," Sorin muttered.

"A toast." Dad held up his glass. "It's amazing. I've two daughters and—"

I shouted over the music. "And one of them has a clairvoyant gift. *One* of them."

"Yeah. Wow," Sorin shouted. "What are the odds?"

Sorin was such a bad actor.

I punched out some animated cheer. "Incredible Thomasina has such abilities. Amazing."

"Val, I didn't know you were so excited about my gift."

"I'm excited about everything to do with you."

"As you should be. We're now best friends."

No. Sorin was my best friend. She'd learn.

"You know, kids, I always felt your mom had some sort of special gift." Dad downed the remainder of his drink and then pointed to the painting of Gisella across the room. "She always denied it. She claimed, she just cared about people."

"Daddy, that doesn't make any sense. Caring about people doesn't make you psychic."

"Thomasina, your mother believed if somebody cared and listened with their ears and with their heart, they'd know what to say or do, to help a person feel better. She felt that's what made the in-tune, caring person appear psychic."

"Or gifted."

"Yes, Val. Girls, your mother cared about others and knew how to make people feel better. It was her gift. I asked her about it, asked her if she was some sort of healer. She said, no. She believed when you cared about others, your sensitivity and intuition naturally grew." Dad sighed. "You're just like her."

"Daddy, I'm over here. Why are you staring at Valthea? *I'm* the special one, the one with the gift."

"Thomasina." Dad shifted on the couch to face her. "You're both my daughters, equally gifted, special and loved."

"But I'm more like mum. They say clairvoyance runs in families."

Who was *they*? Did my sister just make stuff up as needed?

"Thomasina." Dad rubbed his hands together. "Why don't you explain what the pink ring around Val means? And then, how about reading Sorin and my auras? Or is aura seeing and interpreting draining?"

"It is, Daddy. It's incredibly draining."

"Oh brother," Sorin mumbled under his breath.

I took my second sip of the chilled, anise-flavored sambuca. "Dad. How come you never told me that you thought my mom was healer or whatever?"

"You mean, *our* mum." Thomasina waved one finger back and forth from me to her.

"We talked about her sensitivity. I'm sorry. I thought I told you."

"It's okay. I just want to know everything about her." But it wasn't okay. I wanted to be the first one to know anything and everything to do with our mother. After all, my whole life, I had her all to myself.

"Have you always been able to read auras?" Dad asked.

"Yes, but as a child, I thought everyone saw colors around people. I didn't know it was a unique gift until I was nine." She tapped her watch. "It's almost ten. Let's do some family photos before we get too tired. We'll talk about everybody's auras tomorrow." She headed over to the foyer table and removed a camera from her tote bag. "Plus, I've a job interview in the morning."

"Already?" Ambitious. "That's fantastic. What time? One of us can give you a ride."

"It's okay." Thomasina kept messing with her camera. "I'm using Daddy's car."

"Where to?" Sorin set his drink on the coffee table and stood.

"Daddy can decide. I'll work with the lighting in the room."

"No, I mean where's your interview?"

"I'm a bit superstitious. I'll tell everyone afterward."

"I understand. Stay focused. It'll go well." Dad removed the vase of two-dozen burgundy roses, sitting on the round table in front of the garnet wall. He carefully placed them on the coffee table and then walked back to the table. "Sorin, help me move this out of the way. I want to do the photos here, with us standing next to Gisella's portrait."

Grama Alessia said the artist painted the piece from a photo taken on the night of my mother's sixteenth birthday party. The night she and my dad met. Grama wanted my dad to have the painting. She said the light in my mom's eyes reflected her falling in love with him that night. Dad kept it in its original ornate frame.

"Dad. It's weird to stand in front of a painting."

Thomasina spun around. "I can make it work."

"Okay. You're the photographer."

They moved the table away from the wall. Dad tucked in his shirt. "Thomasina, when you read auras you know what people are feeling. That's got to have its advantages."

Although Dad didn't catch her roll her eyes at his question, I did.

"It helps me understand people, Daddy." She shut off the overhead track lighting and turned on one table lamp and one standing floor light. "Reading auras is a skill. Interpreting details of the colors are a gift. It isn't something I'd ever abuse."

My sister's aura-reading skills appeared to be above average. Which meant, I needed to safeguard against Thomasina's moodiness. I needed to be aware of my emotions when hanging out with her. Seeing auras allowed my sister to know things at any given second. Me? I had to wait for a past vision. And so far, with her, there'd been few. To win the mental battle with my twin, I needed to stay calm and centered. We weren't in a battle. But just in case.

"Sorin," I whispered. "I *need* to read her. Get some sort of past vision."

"Babe, you can't wait for, or depend on, a vision. Why don't you talk to her, or pray for insight?"

"I have prayed. Normally, I would've had five to six insights by now. I've never had this much trouble reading anyone."

"Yeah, you have."

Apollonia.

Ten

I sat up, wide awake with a brilliant idea. Two-thirty-eight am. A panel of moonlight shot from our bedroom's balcony window onto the floor. I tiptoed across the white beam, went into the den, and wrote out my idea, sketched costumes, and titled the potential show theme.

Sorin brewed a full pot of strong coffee. I scrambled some eggs and burnt the rye toast. I offered to re-do the toast, but Sorin said he liked it that way. We sat together at the breakfast bar, facing the gulf.

"I'm going to school early again today." Sorin hit his eggs with a few shots of tabasco sauce. "The main acupuncture professor will choose his assistant soon. I'm hoping my devotion to class, thorough attention to detail, and amiable personality, make me the best candidate to assist Dr. Xiong." He flipped up his collar and exaggerated finger combing his hair back.

"Leave the collar up. That'll definitely win them over."

"Wishful thinking." He folded his collar down. "The other teachers and their assistants watch how the newer students act and interact with each other and the teaching staff. Everybody at school wants a smooth-sailing ship." He slathered more jam on his toast.

"Sounds like the circus. Nobody wants troublesome divas." I sipped my coffee. "That's a lot of jam. Guess you do love your toast burnt."

"I don't draw the line until the black part crumbles to dust before I can eat it." He exaggerated biting into his toast.

My Auntie Sylvie used to say, Sorin *tickled* her. She also used to say, a couple stayed in-love if they maintained trust, intimacy, and a sense of humor.

"Val, how'd you sleep? You got up in the middle of the night."

"Yes, I'm so excited. An idea came to me for the student's show."

"That's terrific. I want to hear all about, but first, there's something I need to get off my chest."

My stomach panged. I thought we were in love. I thought everything between us was grand. I thought—

"It's Thomasina."

My stomach calmed.

"I feel like she has you and Dad wrapped around her finger. I don't believe her intentions are sincere. She acts coy and stupid around Dad, and around you, she acts like you're her long-lost, best friend."

"We are long-lost sisters. I'm not entangled in her web of manipulations. Thomasina just found her biological family. I know what it's like. She'll stop spinning out of control and settle down. Hey, you're not jealous of her, are you?"

"You girls stay up late talking. She and Dad come over every morning for coffee. Every night, the four of us eat dinner together. Val, I'm all about family, but we haven't had much alone time since she's arrived."

"That's one reason I love you. You're about us. Okay. I promise we'll keep our precious, quality time."

"I also don't want you to get hurt. I know how badly you want family. Please, try to see people for who they really are."

"I do, and I will. Hello. I read people, remember?"

"Yeah, except for Thomasina."

"I don't need to be psychic to know things."

He scooted closer and put his arms around my waist. "You are a pretty wise girl."

"Pretty wise, or pretty and wise?"

"See what I mean? You're both." He kissed me with the kind of passion America's *Hallmark* TV movies kept behind closed doors.

I whispered, "Nice. What time do you come home tonight?"

"Not soon enough. Now tell me all about your idea, babe." He bit into his burnt toast. Charred crumbs fell to his plate.

I took a swig of my coffee. "All right. My idea is for the theme of Cirque du Palm's student spring show. The production must include enough acts and roles to involve students from beginning to advanced, plus, show off lots of beautiful costumes."

"Naturally. What's the title?"

I held up my hands, as if presenting a marquee. "Circtopia."

"A circus in a utopian world? I like it."

"Actually, dystopian world."

"Even better."

"The story follows an orphaned, fifteen-year-old boy, living in a dismal, dystopian society, and his quest to become a famous high-wire artist. He auditions for a coveted spot in his society's prestigious circus. Auditions takes place in a circus-ring, far from friendly. The competition plays out like a brutal battle."

"That's heavy."

"Exactly. Acceptance into Circtopia guarantees safety and privilege, luxury lodging and delicious food, for all performers and crew. But at the end of Circtopia's season, the ringmaster, who's also the city's dictator, tosses the old cast back into their life of scarcity, and auditions fresh talent."

"The teen wire-walker makes the cut, right?"

"Yes, after battling a ruthless competitor, also vying for the high-wire spot." I took a bite of eggs.

Sorin put down his fork.

My toast wasn't burnt and tasted scrumptious with a locally-made orange marmalade.

"Val?"

"What?"

"You can't stop there. What happens next? How does the story end?"

"I can't tell you."

"Why not?"

"Because, I want you to wait and come to the show."

"I can't wait that long."

"Don't you love the smell of this marmalade's sweet tartness blended with our hazelnut coffee?"

"Don't try to change the subject."

"Why not? It's so delicious."

"I don't know if you're talking about our breakfast or how you're driving me crazy."

"More coffee?"

"Okay. Your story's great. Unusual for circus. Dark. Edgy. Alberto will choose your idea. It's unique. Come on, tell me about your wire-walker's contender. How evil's the guy?"

"It's not a guy. It's his sister."

That night, Sorin stopped for Thai takeout on his way home from acupuncture school. We brought it over to Dad's. After dinner, Thomasina gathered us in the living room.

"Thanks for dinner, Sorin."

"Yes, thank you, Son. But remember, I'm still cooking Romanian food at least once a week."

"And I'm helping, Daddy, right?"

"Right."

Thomasina didn't offer Dad his favorite spot on his sectional couch, but instead, plopped her derriere down on the left end, reclining seat. "Have a seat, everyone."

Another example of how my twin and I weren't identical. Dad sat next to her, and Sorin and I sat next to him.

"I'll continue with the auras where we left off last night. Or Daddy, do you first want to share about your new adventure?"

"What new adventure?" Sorin asked.

"Tell you in a bit. Let's do the aura stuff first."

Thomasina put on an affected hush whenever speaking about auras. "As you recall, I told you I saw some pink and other colors around Valthea. Now, let's go on and talk about Sorin."

"Wait." Sorin leaned forward. "You never said what her pink meant."

"Pink is a nice aura color."

Nice? That's it? Why wouldn't my sister elaborate—

"Going on. Sorin, around you, there's dark green, royal blue, some pink, and a few sprays of white. It's an easy interpretation. You were born to be in the healing arts, a doctor, acupuncturist, whatever. You're good-hearted and brilliant."

I snuggled into Sorin. "See. I've been telling you that forever."

"That's right, babe." He kissed my head, or rather, my ponytail. "How about that? And you don't even read auras."

"Thomasina's exactly right about you, Son. I always knew you were going to go into medicine."

"Dad, what are you talking about? Since I was a kid, you pushed me to take over The Gypsy Royales."

"I pushed it on you to force you to defend your heart's desire. When Apollonia brought you home after finding—"

"—kidnapping me."

"What?" Thomasina gasped.

"Sorin, I told you a million times. You came into our lives, an adorable little boy with a toy stethoscope around your neck. It was obvious. You were destined to be a doctor." Dad paused. "I knew, deep down, you'd eventually choose to follow in your biological father's footsteps."

"Wait." Thomasina faced Dad. "Sorin's father was a doctor? I don't know this story—"

"We don't know for sure if he was a doctor. Anyway, another time." Sorin sat back. "Forget about me. Do my Dad's colors."

"Except, Sorin, I'm not done with you." Thomasina slid a folder out from under a book on Dad's coffee table. "Here. It's not about your aura. But it'll help how one of your teachers view you."

"What is it?" He opened the folder.

I looked over his shoulder. "Is that your letter to Dr. Xiong?"

"Yeah but ..." He held up the letter on top, giving it a quick scan. "This is better. Tighter."

"I tried." Thomasina sat back, kicking out the foot rest of her seat. "This morning, you left the letter on the kitchen island. I saw it was addressed to a doctor at your school. I took the liberty of tidying your English grammar and sentence structure. It reads more assertive, but quite pleasant." She shrugged. "You don't have to use it. Your original's there, too. Are you upset? It was lying out in the open. You mentioned the other night that you really want to be chosen as your teacher's assistant. I think my letter will help you. But, it's your choice. Submit either one."

Sorin held both letters up, studying them. "Yours is much better. You're obviously more experienced with English. Thanks, Thomasina." He put them back into the folder. "It was nice of you. But, next time, ask us before taking documents or whatever we may have laying out."

"Come on, Son. Don't be so uptight." Dad lounged back and put his socked feet on the coffee table. "Your sister was just trying to help."

"Sister-in-law. And I know. I said, thank you. But in the future—"

"I stopped *everything* I was doing, because I wanted to help you." Thomasina sat forward, closing the foot stool. "You want the assistant position. I wanted to surprise you in a positive way. After all, you've been so patient and accepting of me."

"I said, thank you, Thomasina."

"You're welcome again. Now let's focus on Daddy." She plucked a dark chocolate mint from the candy dish in the center of the coffee table. "Daddy's aura has bright yellow, bits of red, orange, violet. He has boundless energy and passion."

"Yes, yes, you're so good. That's exactly how I feel."

"Gee, Dad, didn't the lady at the deli tell you the same thing last week?"

"Son, that lady said those things because she saw the Cirque du Palm logo on my shirt. The crew told me, she's tried for years to cater the circus's events. Her flattery covered her agenda." He grinned. "Thomasina doesn't guess. She knows the truth. Plus, she has no agenda."

"But I do."

Pin drop.

She giggled too throaty for her ingenue facial expression. "I want your love and acceptance."

"Such a sweet girl."

"Oh brother," Sorin mumbled under his breath.

Oh sister. Thomasina treated reading auras like a parlor game.

"Daddy, I need to tell you something. There's a black splotch over part of your heart. But, thanks to me, that splotch's about to disappear. Sorin, Valthea, are you ready for some ace news?"

"Sure," I said, dry as possible.

Sorin bumped his shoulder to Dad's. "Are you blushing?"

"I don't know, but I am excited."

"You tell them, Daddy."

"All right." Dad clasped his hands together. "This morning—"

"I'll tell them." Thomasina sat forward. "This morning, I signed Daddy up for three different Internet dating sites. This afternoon, he met a woman for coffee."

"Way to go, Dad." Sorin slapped him a high five. "Finally."

"What? You already met someone in person?"

"Come on, Dad. Tell us. What does she look like? Did she fall in love with you yet?"

"Or did you fall in love with her?"

"Easy, kids." Dad fidgeted with his panther ring. "Colleen is a pretty and kind lady. I asked her on a second date."

"That's awesome, Dad."

Thomasina stretched out on the recliner like a queen.

In less than three weeks, my sister linked herself to the lives of the two most important men in my life. Yes, Cosmo Dobra was her father, and Sorin Dobra was her brother-in-law. But up until now, I was the only girl in the mix.

"Dad, show us your profile. Is it sufficiently macho?"

"Sorin. Macho?"

"Hold on. I'll show you." Thomasina turned on her iPad, tapped an app, and in ten-seconds, adjusted her tablet to face us. "Check it out. One headshot. Three full photos."

Sorin pointed. "Handstand on a fence. That's the best. It shows the crazy you."

"I like the one of us gathered around the Christmas tree at your home in Brasov last year."

"I prefer this one, Val." Thomasina used two fingers to expand the photo of her and Dad playing frisbee on the beach."

"Who took the picture?" Sorin asked. "And, Dad. How many ladies have written to you? Or do you write to them?"

"A passerby took the photo." Thomasina beamed. "And a lot of ladies have already expressed interest in our Dad. He also wrote to some choice babes."

"I have?"

"I wrote for you, Daddy."

Sorin touched the I-Pad screen, scrolling down a bit. "Dad. You checked the highest income box. $150,000.00 and above. You don't earn that anymore."

"I didn't fill that part out."

"I did. Listen, Daddy does well. He's successful."

I wondered if Dad told Thomasina about the bank account we opened for him. I never wanted my father to ask me for money. After all, I was the one who begged him to come to

America and leave the troupe. If my grandfather hadn't kept my mother from marrying him, she would've left him everything.

"Thomasina, don't you think checking the box of a high income draws gold-diggers?"

"Sorin, they're over forty. It's okay if a woman wants to meet a confident, successful man, and vice versa."

Dad sat back. "Feels silly putting pictures online for anyone in the world to see."

"Daddy, it's normal, these days. You haven't allowed yourself to fall in love in almost twenty years. Although it took a lot of work on my part, you're now open to the idea. There's no turning back." Thomasina continued searching for something on her tablet.

"You're right." Dad shook his head. "I don't need to feel guilty or afraid anymore."

"Found her." Thomasina passed her tablet around. "This is the woman Daddy met today."

"She's nice-looking, Dad. Way to go."

I couldn't believe my eyes. "Uh, Dad, doesn't she resemble someone?"

"No." Thomasina snap-closed her tablet case and kicked in the foot rest. She glanced at Dad's cell phone vibrating on the coffee table. "Perfect timing. Comb your hair, Dad."

"Why?" Dad picked up his phone. "Evening, Aaron. How are you—what?" Dad hopped off the couch. "Now? Okay. Thanks. Send her up." He ran to the wall mirror and finger-combed his hair. "She's here."

"Who?" Sorin and I asked.

"Colleen." Thomasina stood at the front door. "Daddy, I hope you don't mind. I invited her over for dessert. Or rather, you did. I wrote to her pretending to be you. You can be a bit shy."

"My dad isn't shy. Why don't you try honesty instead of sneakiness?"

C.K. Mallick

"Our dad." Thomasina lit the cherry blossom candle setting on the foyer table. "I'll tell Colleen the truth. And we Brits are called uptight buggers. Relax, Sorin. It's just tea and dessert."

"Thomasina, he's not uptight. He's honest. There's a difference. We'll talk about that later. First, do we have any dessert to serve?"

"Sissy, please. I've everything under control. The dining room's set. Tea's brewing. Three decadent desserts on platters await."

"How do I look?" Dad wiped his brow.

"Handsome as ever." I straightened the shoulder seams of his sweater. "Uh, Dad. Doesn't Colleen remind you of —"

The doorbell rang. He rushed toward the door.

I stood next to Sorin, behind Dad and Thomasina.

Sorin put his arm around my waist. "Your sister's completely out of control."

"Yes, she is. But at least Dad's meeting people."

"Hi. You must be Colleen." Thomasina ushered in the petite, forty-something woman. "I'm Thomasina. You've probably heard a lot about me."

"Yes, Thomasina. It's nice to meet you." The strawberry-blonde spoke softly. She'd a sweet smile. She stepped past Thomasina. "Hello, Cosmo. Thank you so much for inviting me over tonight."

"Good evening, Colleen."

Thomasina didn't move out of their way.

Dad stepped around Thomasina. He took Colleen's hand in his and kissed it. "Thank you for coming. I couldn't have waited another day to see you."

"Me either." She blushed.

Sorin whispered, "I'd say, Dad's smitten."

Dad and Miss Colleen turned, facing Sorin and me. "You've met Thomasina. Now meet Sorin and Valthea."

116

"Hi, Miss Colleen. I'm Valthea. It's wonderful to meet you."

"Thank you, Valthea. I'm delighted to meet you. I've heard many wonderful things about you, including your upcoming American debut." Her tourmaline green eyes sparkled.

"Thank you. Dad often exaggerates, except about how beautiful you are."

"Aw, thank you. And you're Sorin."

"Good evening Miss Colleen."

"Your father told me all about you. He's so proud of everything you've accomplished."

"Thank you. I'm proud of him, too." He winked at Dad.

"I'm sorry to stare, Miss Colleen," I said. "It's just that you remind me of someone we know. Doesn't Miss Colleen remind you of someone you used to know?"

"No." Dad shrugged. "Not really."

Love was blind and clueless.

"They do say everyone has a twin. Valthea, please tell me. Who do I resemble?"

"A woman named Gisella."

Dad's face paled.

"I do hope she's someone you all like."

"Yes," I said. "She was loved by all."

Eleven

My two-hour rehearsal time slot in the show tent was nearly up. I climbed down the rope hanging next to my rings and grabbed my towel and phone from my gym bag. I texted Dad. "Want to meet for lunch?"

My new life in Florida was grand. Morning included a water view breakfast and Sorin. I practiced the Roman Rings five days a week at the Cirque du Palm tent. I taught the silks, Lyra, and web to the circus art students three nights a week and on Saturdays. Lunchtime sometimes included Dad, Thomasina, or my circus hero, Romeo Bach. My family broke bread together at night, often over Romanian food. Sorin and I reserved one night a week for date night. All was well. My past world and my new world melded together.

Dad texted back. "Next time. Lunch plans with Colleen."

"Have fun. See you tonight."

"Dinner and movie with Colleen," he texted. "Catch you after, if you're still up."

"OK. Tell her hi." Guess he really liked Colleen. At least he finally admitted the resemblance between her and my mom. I texted Thomasina, "Meet for lunch?"

She texted back, "I've an interview, but can meet at one-ish?"

"Sure. Good luck." She didn't say anything about an interview this morning.

She texted again. "Meet you at Veg-Out."

"Perfect."

Romeo and his crew entered the arena.

I carried my gym bag out of the ring, waving to him. He had the next rehearsal time slot.

Romeo waved back, but his laser-focus told me he was already in the zone. The gold letters on his black t-shirt read,

C.K. Mallick

I Dare. I Dare was Romeo's trademark phrase and the title of his upcoming bio.

I sat in the stands, honored to be part of such a show. I planned on watching Romeo rehearse while reviewing my notes for *Circtopia*. If Alberto chose *Circtopia* as the youth's spring show, it'd be my big break into assisting him in the future. I pulled my spiral notebook, index cards, and colored markers from my gym bag. Where was my folder with all my notes?

A text came through from Sorin on my phone. "Keep your fingers crossed. I overheard Dr. Xiong talking to another teacher. He favors me for assistant. Maybe Thomasina's letter helped."

I texted back. "You're the perfect candidate, with or without her version of your letter. You'll get it."

"Thanks. Talk tonight. XOXO"

"XOXO" I set my phone down. Where'd I leave that folder? We both wanted to be assistants.

The dynamic, classical piece of music, Sabre Dance shot out from an I-pod speaker. At the same time, a three-foot-round cupcake with pink frosting and a candle on top, scuttled in and around the circus ring. Suddenly, one of the cupcake's sides poked out and then the other. The pokes alternated in time with the striking music. Picturing Romeo scrunched inside the cupcake made me laugh. After a little more comedic struggle, Romeo crawled out of the cupcake triumphant. He drew the candle from the top of it and commenced in a one-sided swordfight with his frosted enemy.

A fifteen-foot-long, black-and-white cake rolled to the downstage center of the ring. Romeo dropped his candle sword and sprinted to the four-foot-high, black-and-white cake. He climbed up one side and dove into its center. Instead of the cake swallowing him up, he rebounded. He sprung ten feet into the air. A small trampoline hid at the base of the cake's structure, out of the audience's view. Every time Romeo sprung into the air, he struck a funny pose or turned a flip.

I hadn't jumped on a trampoline in years. It's funny that when you watch someone fly through the air in an act or a stunt, it makes you feel free. Why was that?

Four crew guys pushed a sixty-two-foot tall, six tier Godzilla cake behind the trampoline. Romeo spotted the greyish-green Godzilla cake while flying in the air. He screamed and then fumbled — on purpose — landing draped over the edge of the black-and-white cake. He peeled himself off the trampoline cake and held his arms up in surrender to Godzilla. A five-foot tall, number twenty candle topped the monster cake.

Romeo's reactions cracked me up more than his actions. Until I remembered, I'd no idea where I left my *Circtopia* folder. I had typed all my notes and printed the pages that morning. The pages went in a binder either on the kitchen island or in my gymbag.

After several hilarious bouts of Romeo Bach meets Godzilla cake encounters, Romeo whistled to his crew guys for help. One came running. He handed Romeo a Swiss Alpine-style hat and two hiking poles. Romeo strapped a mountain climber's belt around his waist, double checked its fastening, and then initiated the audience in an even clap beat. His audience today was two people sitting near the top row and me. We kept the beat going as he scaled Godzilla's six-tiers.

We applauded when he made it to the top.

Romeo put on an arrogant, cocky air. He threw down his hat and hiking poles and then struck a body builder pose. Instead of holding the pose, he slipped. He yelped, toppling from the cake, but then flew. Romeo Bach flew around the ring suspended by wires. He acted afraid and alarmed at first, but then waved and laughed. He finished sailing through the air, mimicking swimming the breast stroke. The actual show included a club mix of the song, Happy Birthday, a disco ball, and swirling confetti lighting.

C.K. Mallick

Five minutes later, I met Romeo at the edge of the ring. "Bravo." I cheered. "So clever. Your act gets better every time you do it."

"Thanks. Did you laugh a little or a lot?"

"A lot. I'm surprised you couldn't hear me. That act energizes me."

"Good. Good." He yelled to his crew guys, rolling the Godzilla cake out of the ring, "Let's set up and do it again." He pulled off his sweatband. "You sticking around?"

"Yeah, I'm waiting to meet my sister for lunch at one. I'm fine-tuning some notes on my idea for Alberto's theme meeting tomorrow."

"I heard about the meeting. What's your idea?"

My heart sped, honored by Romeo Bach's interest. "I'll tell you. But please, don't tell anyone, not Alberto, Thomasina, or your crew guys. Only Sorin knows."

"Yes ma'am." He saluted and then relaxed.

"I call it, *Circtopia*. It's about boy in a dystopian society who competes in a battle-like audition to be in the town's coveted circus, which guarantees performers and their families food and safety for one circus season."

"That's sensational. Alberto will love it."

"Thanks. I hope he also likes the contrast I sketched out for the props and costumes."

"What contrast?"

"The grim brown of the dystopian society versus the over the top, colorful circus world."

"Sounds unique. I like it. It's fresh."

"Thanks. Hopefully, Alberto will think so, too."

"Hey, Val. You want to invite me go to lunch with you and your sister?"

Twelve

The downtown Sarasota restaurant called Veg-Out offered gourmet fresh food and the excitement of weekday bustle from eleven to three. It won the Sarasota's Best competition for vegan restaurant. Residents and tourists packed the place. I chose one of the back tables for four. The décor's counterbalance of marigold, pimento, and lime green, hit with patches of black-and-white check print, added to its whimsical charm. Framed photographs hung on the marigold wall next to me. My three favorites included the little boy amused by a hopping baby goat, the curly-haired girl offering a daisy to a knock-kneed calf, and the boy in an oversized sweater, cradling a gray bunny.

The waitress poured water into the glasses on the table.

I stopped her after three. "Thank you. They'll just be three of us."

"All right. I'll check back with you." She laid three menus on the tables.

The menu offered six lunch choices. I stared at it. Where would Sorin and I raise our children? Florida? Bucharest? Somewhere else?

"Hi, Val."

"Thomasina."

"I've been standing here for two seconds." She set her purse on one of the chairs. "You must really love something on that menu." She smoothed her sleeveless, mini navy dress and sat. A sheer-fuchsia wrap draped over her shoulders.

"Thomasina, you look pretty. It's so European, your dressing up for lunch."

"I didn't have time to go home. I came straight here."

"You wore that to a job interview?"

"Val. Navy's classic. Everybody knows that."

Everybody also knows, tight, short dresses are inappropriate in the work place. "How did it go?"

"My meeting went much better than expected."

"Meeting? I thought it was a job interview."

"I don't want to talk about it. You'll jinx it. I got your second text. I don't know why we couldn't have lunch alone." Thomasina stopped the waitress walking by. "What is today's ice tea?"

"Today, we've cocoa peppermint or peach melon."

"I'll take the cocoa mint, please. Val?"

"Peach melon. Thank you."

"I'll let your waitress know."

I spotted Romeo walking toward us from the entrance. Perfect posture. Athletic physique. Clean cut good looks.

Several ladies sitting at the juice bar and high-top tables turned their heads.

He snuck up behind Thomasina. He stopped one foot behind her chair. He pressed his index finger to his lips.

I obliged and played along. You can take the daredevil clown out of the circus, but you can't take the circus out of the —

"Blimey." Thomasina flipped over her menu. "I can't believe you invited a clown to join us for lunch."

Romeo held his position.

"Thomasina. Romeo Bach is world famous. He's a daredevil comic. He does tons of risky stunts."

"Fine, Val. But tell me the truth. Is he creepy?"

I tried like a ventriloquist to keep my mouth still. "Shhh."

"I don't mind you in tights and makeup, but a guy?"

"Afternoon, ladies." Romeo stepped out from behind Thomasina.

Thomasina did a double take. "Oh." She looked him up and down. "Well. Hello to you, too."

How embarrassing. Why didn't she just slurp him up on the spot. "Hi, Romeo. Glad you could make it." I think. "This is my sister. Thomasina Stratham. Thomasina, this is Romeo Bach."

Thomasina scooted out of her chair and stood, accidently bumping into Romeo's chest. "Sorry about that."

"You okay?"

"Nice to meet you, Mr. Bach." She held out her hand.

He kissed the back of it. "Lovely to meet you. Please, call me, Romeo." He sat in the chair closest her.

"I've never met a clown before."

"I'm a daredevil, who has fun."

"If you say so. Mr. Bach." She half-smiled.

"I do. Miss Stratham."

What was wrong with these two? "Waitress will be right back."

"Okay. Great." Romeo glanced at Thomasina's dress and then quickly looked at her face.

"Mr. Bach. You're glad you joined us for lunch, aren't you?"

"Just like you're glad that I didn't wear makeup and tights to lunch. Less creepy that way, Miss Stratham. Don't you think?"

Touché, Romeo.

Thomasina unknotted her wrap. The silk scarf slipped off her shoulders and onto to the floor.

Romeo retrieved it in a flash.

"Thank you, Mr. Bach," she purred. "You're such a gentle-man." She took the scarf. Her fingers lingered around his.

"Your welcome. Miss Stratham." Romeo's Swiss white skin flushed at the cheeks.

Where was our waitress to break the tension?

"By the way, Mr. Bach ..." Thomasina didn't cover her shoulders and deep neckline with the scarf, as she wore it before. She draped it over the back of her chair. "I knew you were behind me when I was talking about you."

No, she didn't.

"But good news, Mr. Bach. You passed the test. You proved yourself confident and unflinching."

"Except, I don't believe you knew I stood behind you." He grinned. "No worries, Miss Stratham. You passed my test. You recovered your pose. Certain assets distract."

"Toasty in here, isn't it?" I peeled off my suede, zip up jacket.

Thomasina brushed her hair from her shoulder. "Mr. Bach. I'm afraid you did not know that I knew you were there. But I fancy your complimentary deduction. So, I'll take it."

"Miss Stratham. I'm afraid, you can't take it. I already gave it to you."

I went from feeling invisible to feeling like an intruder. Thank goodness, the waitress walked up.

"Hi there. What would you like to drink, sir?"

"Mr. Bach." Thomasina wrapped her hand around Romeo's bicep and then pulled him near her. "I've a suggestion."

Yeah, so do I. Go get a hotel room.

Romeo leaned in close to her voluptuousness. "Yes, Miss Stratham?"

"Ginger tonic smoothie. Good for a man's virility. Plus, it's ice cold."

"I'm good on virility, but I do need to cool down."

"One ginger tonic smoothie, please."

"Yes, sir." The waitress winked and then took our order.

Sparks and banter continued to fly between Thomasina and Romeo for the next fifteen minutes. Finally, the waitress served our food, interrupting their endless tennis volley.

Romeo opened his hands to each of us. "I'd like to pray before we eat."

I put my fork down. "Me, too." I took his hand and opened my other for Thomasina.

Thomasina set down her ice tea.

"Miss Stratham. Are you a Christian?" he asked.

"Ugh, Mr. Bach. Must you ruin our meal and upbeat mood with a question like that? What's your point? Romeo Bach. What a weird choice for a stage name."

"Romeo Bach is my real name. My mother comes from the Italian section of Switzerland. And thank you." He took back the hand he'd offered her. "Your non-answer answers my question."

Blasted Thomasina.

"Please, Romeo, don't be so tough on me." Thomasina squirmed. "I'm English, remember? I grew up with heavy, dragging church hymns. Tongue twisting King James. And don't forget, way too much rain." She straightened the napkin on her lap for the third time. "I want to be a chipper. A happy believer, like you. But I don't how. I obviously need help. Suggestions?" She offered her hand for prayer.

Did my sister seek the spiritual, or was she playing Romeo?

"Let's keep it simple. We'll give thanks that we have food to eat." Romeo bowed his head. He gave thanks and blessed the food.

After the waitress cleared our plates, she served our colorful, vegan desserts. We ordered three to share. Pink lemonade meringue pie. Orange and chocolate cheesecake with edible flowers. Tahini Coconut Fudge.

"Mr. Bach. I need to tell you something."

"Yes, Miss Stratham. What is it?"

Back to that? "Try some dessert, guys." I ate one of the flowers.

"I see auras. But don't judge me. I'm not a witch."

"I don't judge."

I ate a corner of the coconut fudge. "Try the fudge. It's divine."

"But, if I was a witch, Mr. Bach, would you date me?" Thomasina held a forkful of the meringue pie up to Romeo's mouth.

He'd no choice. He opened his mouth, and she fed him the bites of pie. He chewed and swallowed. "No, Miss Stratham. I wouldn't."

"So, you are judgmental."

"No." He fed her a piece of cheesecake. "I simply prefer not to waste time dating someone unless there's a potential future."

"You're completely predictable."

"No, Miss Stratham. You're the predictable one."

I sat back, nibbling on my piece of fudge, ducking out of the line of fire.

"If you read auras, like you say you do—"

"Are you calling me a liar?"

"No, Miss Stratham. But you sort of behave like a spoiled, teen girl."

Thomasina retracted the bite of fudge she held near Romeo's mouth and dropped it onto her plate. "Valthea."

"Yes?"

"Are all daredevil comics arrogant and insulting? Or just this one?"

"I don't think Romeo meant—"

"Allow me to rephrase. Miss Stratham, it seems you use your manner, looks, and maybe your color reading to get what you want and control situations and people. Just because someone has the extra-sensory ability to read or see things about a person, doesn't give them the right to dive into their head and see things."

"It's not like that," I said.

"Thanks, Val. But I can stick up for myself."

I nodded, feeling my cheeks flush. I never meant to dive into anyone's mind. Visions just showed up.

"Mr. Bach, auras reveal the true person. Who they are, isn't my fault. I think you're jealous because I'm at an advantage. Plus, I draw attention wherever I go. People don't even know who you are unless you're wearing your circus garb and clown makeup."

"You both drew attention walking in here today."

"Thanks for the diplomacy," Thomasina snarled.

"Miss Stratham. I don't need attention outside the ring."

"If you say so." She chewed up a petunia.

"I say, we get some to-go boxes." I looked around for our waitress.

"Miss Stratham, you act like you know what everyone's about. What they're going to say. You categorize and dismiss people as quick as possible, so they never have a chance to figure you out."

Thomasina's stoic expression turned furious. She tossed her napkin on her plate and scooted back in her chair. "Is this how American Christians act?"

Romeo leaned toward her, half-whispering. "I'm just being honest."

I heard every word.

"Miss Stratham, your defensive attitude doesn't protect you. It actually keeps happiness from you." He shook his head. "Boasting is overcompensation for insecurity. I don't know your past, but do you really want to lug a steel-plated shield and sword around with you everywhere?"

"Now, who thinks they know everything?" Thomasina spoke loud enough for the ladies at the high-top tables to hear.

"Let's finish this conversation outside." I waved for our waitress. "I'll get the bill."

"The check's all set, Val. I took care of it earlier."

"Romeo. I invited you to lunch."

"Technically, I invited myself. Plus, I'm old-fashioned that way."

"Well, thank you so much."

Thomasina pulled her wrap over her shoulders. "Yes. Thank you."

"You're welcome, ladies. Miss Stratham, do you like flowers? Gardens? Banyan trees? Beautiful scenery?"

"Mr. Bach, I'm from England. We live for gardens. What does that have to do with anything?"

I stood, anxious to exit before another loud volley.

Romeo held my chair.

"Thank you." His patience with Thomasina impressed me. It matched my own.

He held Thomasina's chair.

She picked up her handbag and stepped in front of him.

"Accept my invitation to one of Sarasota's premier spots. The Selby Gardens. And bring your camera. It's a photographer's dream."

Thomasina blinked several times, as if confused or dumbfounded. I couldn't read auras, but I knew she was thrilled.

"I'll pick you up Saturday morning. Nine thirty."

Romeo Bach. Daredevil comic. Patient man. Smooth operator.

Thomasina led the way out. "Nine forty-five."

Romeo waited. "Valthea, your sister is as crazy about me as I am her."

Thirteen

I sped, racing around the last block, to arrive early at the Cirque du Palm arena. Europeans drove faster than Americans, but things happened faster in America. Like with my family.

Dad and Colleen met up every day for the past week. Dr. Xiong told Sorin he was the top candidate for his assistant. Alberto granted Thomasina permission to photograph Saturday's kid classes. My solo act progressed, as did my friendship with Romeo Bach. Thomasina hadn't spewed out any poison in days. Maybe all she needed was love. She and Romeo had been inseparable since Selby Gardens. Sorin continued his enthusiasm about starting a family in a couple of years. I believed in my show theme, *Circtopia*.

I parked next to Thomasina's rental. She must've been taking pictures of Romeo. I walked into the arena.

In the center of the ring, Romeo climbed up the last ten feet of a sixty-foot-high, sway pole. As he climbed the sway pole, it did exactly that—sway. Two crewmen stood on other side. They spotted him in case, well, in case.

I joined Thomasina, seated in the front row. "Hey, Sis."

"I can't talk. I've never seen such an act. I can't watch."

Non-circus folk. "Thomasina, you have to watch. He's your friend."

"Aye," Romeo cried out, losing his grip.

"No!" Thomasina covered her eyes.

Romeo slipped and now hung from one hand, with his legs dangling under him.

She pointed. "Somebody help him."

I played along, shouting, "Hang on, Romeo."

Romeo's spotters hustled to the right and left as needed. Romeo reached for the pole but missed. He wrapped his legs around the pole, but then his other hand slipped.

Thomasina screamed.

Romeo shot his arms side, keeping his legs wrapped tight. He shouted, "*Voila*."

I applauded, wise to his act's fake out.

"Val, you knew?"

"Sorry. Show biz."

She shouted. "Hey, Bach. Not funny."

"Sorry, Thomasina," Romeo laughed. His crew guy lowered him. He landed and then unfastened his harness.

"It's circus, Thomasina," I said. "We have to entertain." I studied her suit jacket. "Are you wearing the same suit that I'm wearing, but in navy?" She paired her skirt and jacket suit with a red, yellow, and blue, circus motif scarf. I should've done something similar. "Did you just come from an interview?"

"No. I'm going to Alberto's creative meeting."

"My meeting?"

"It's not your meeting, Val."

"Kind of. It's for staff. It's our theme meeting."

Romeo walked toward us, wiping his face with a towel. "Sorry, I gave you a little scare. We have to goof and slip occasionally. Our audience thinks what we do's easy. If we don't thrill them, they'll leave at intermission."

Thomasina play hit him. "You worried me. I couldn't tell you were faking."

"I know. Sorry." He shook his head. "Unfortunately, accidents do happen. Performers fall. Cables snap. People end up dead, or worse, crippled for life. Many times, an audience won't know something horrific has happened. The lighting people will direct the lights away from an accident area and spotlight another act. Or they'll focus on a clown who's suddenly interacting with the crowd in the stands."

Thomasina shuddered. "Now I'm going to worry more about you two."

Romeo kissed her cheek. "Worrying doesn't help anything. Health, focus, and double-checking equipment does. Thomasina. Why are you in a business suit?"

"Alberto's meeting."

"Is he hiring you to shoot the show?" He draped his towel over his shoulder.

"We'll see." She glanced at her phone. "Almost time. Better go."

Romeo walked us to the arena exit. "Ladies, if your meeting goes for an hour, I'll be finished here. We can all go to lunch."

Thomasina petted his shoulder. "Or just you and I can go."

"Yeah, you guys go without me. Most likely, Alberto will want to talk to me or go to lunch after the meeting."

"Or, Alberto may want to take me to lunch after the meeting."

I stopped at the arena door. "You? Why —"

"Romeo, can we play lunch by ear?"

"Sure. I'm flexible."

"Pun intended?" She giggled.

"Always."

"Hey, Rome," one of his crew guys yelled. "We're set."

"Be right there." Romeo winked at me. "Val, your idea's a winner. Pitch it with energy. Alberto will love it." He gave Thomasina a peck on the cheek and ran into the ring.

"Thanks, Romeo." I waved.

Thomasina and I headed toward the back entrance of the offices.

"Val, you lied."

"What are you talking about?"

"You said you only shared your idea with Sorin. But it sounds like you told Romeo, too."

"Thomasina, we talked about this over a week ago. Since then, I shared some of it with Romeo. First things first. It's not nice to call people a liar before you have all the facts. I told Romeo the ten second version of my idea. No need to feel left out." I stayed quiet, but no apology came. "Thomasina, why are coming to the meeting? Does Alberto want you to photograph the show? What makes you think he'd take you to lunch today?"

"Maybe as a congratulation."

"For hiring you as a photographer?" Inflated egos keep people out of touch with reality. How convenient. "Romeo wants to have lunch with you today."

"I can have lunch with him any time. I'm reserving today for Alberto."

We walked down the hall to the meeting room, the only office with a big oval table.

"Good. We're the first ones here." Thomasina pushed past me to walk in first.

No British etiquette there.

Red, blue, and yellow bowls of popcorn and candy lined the meeting room's medieval-style table. Red-and-white stripe folders and pens lay square in front of each high back, medieval chair.

"This is perfect." Thomasina sat across from Alberto's seat, at the other head of the table.

Unbelievable. I sat next to her. Didn't matter. I picked up the striped pen in front of me. I'd soon present my first creative idea. And Alberto would love it.

Gina, the youth circus director and Suki, the students' head coach, walked in behind us. We said hi. I introduced them to Thomasina. They sat on the other side of me.

Troy and Simon, the lighting guy and sound guy walked into the room. They both wore blue jeans and wrinkled, button-down shirts. They stopped talking about their outer-space theme idea long enough to say hi. They converged on the other side of the table and munched away on the popcorn and chocolate covered peanuts.

Thomasina slid her striped folder and pen to the side and set her laptop on the table.

"Why'd you bring your laptop? You going to share photos of the students?"

"Not really."

"Sis, you're photography's great. Don't worry. Most likely, Alberto will let you shoot at least some of the spring shows."

"I'm not worried." She put a mint in her mouth.

What was her problem? Thomasina was self-centered, but she could've wished me good luck with my presentation.

Milly, the receptionist walked in and sat to the right of the head chair.

Alberto walked in a minute before meeting time. "Good afternoon, everyone." He sat.

Thomasina should've offered Gina her seat. Let it go. It's just a chair.

Alberto opened his folder. "First, thank you for all the time and energy you've put into creating a theme for the student's spring show. I'm confident all your ideas are spectacular, but as you know, I can only use one. Troy. Simon. Yesterday, you pitched me your outer space idea. I like how your story takes the audience on a journey to outer space and then finishes on a beach. Great twist. Perfect for the holidays in Florida. I'd like to save your idea as a possibility for our year end show."

"Great, sir."

"Totally perfect for the winter show." Troy slapped Simon a high five.

Should I have told Alberto my theme ahead of time? No. Anticipation was best. Surprises illicit emotion. Emotion catapults passion. And I needed Alberto to be passionate about Circtopia.

"Gina. What do you have?" Alberto sat back.

The ex-aerialist from Poland sat board-straight. "Suki and I worked together on a theme. We call it, Around the World with Circus."

Suki passed out a printed collage. "This collage gives you an idea of the flavor, music, costumes, and choreography we'd feature. Our theme would showcase ten different parts of the world."

Milly put on her reading glasses. "This theme welcomes our international visitors as well as our locals. Troy, Simon, this theme is realistic and easy to follow."

A week ago, I printed and bound some creative photos to pass out today. I used a sepia filter for a few photos. The rest showed the artists who made it into *Circtopia*. They were dressed in dazzling, bright costumes and performed amazing acts in spectacular settings.

Everyone studied or at least glanced at Suki's collage. Except for Thomasina.

Alberto tucked the collage into his folder. "The international theme's a pleasant, but old standard. I need young people coming to our shows. They're our future. Thank you, but sorry ladies. I do know whatever we select, you'll make the choreography fit and be fantastic."

"No problem, Alberto." Gina tucked away the extra collage copies. "After all, Suki and I thought of the last three themes for the school's shows."

Suki pushed up her eyeglasses. "Guess it's someone else's turn."

"Mine," Thomasina blurted. "Alberto, may I present my idea next?"

"You have a show idea?" I whispered. "You didn't tell me. I thought you were here as a photographer."

"Go ahead, Thomasina." Alberto smiled.

Hold on. Did Alberto just make goo-goo eyes at my sister?

Thomasina met his eyes. "Thank you, Alberto."

Ew, no. I quickly eyeballed the group. Everyone messed with their cell phones, except Milly. She filled her plastic bowl with candy. Thank goodness, no one else saw the flirtation.

"Thomasina," Alberto spoke in a sweeter than normal tone. "You've shared parts of your idea over the last three days.

You're obviously a passionate woman. That is, passionate about your idea. So, yes. Please, share it with the group." He blotted his forehead with one of the blue paper napkins. It left a swipe of blue on his forehead.

"Thank you, Alberto." She typed something on her laptop.

I could barely breathe. How could Thomasina stoop so low? Why? This was my world. What did she hope to gain?

"Will someone please turn off the lights? I need to project images on the white board behind Alberto."

Troy shut the lights.

Alberto scooted side.

Was Thomasina trying to impress Romeo? Make me jealous? Push her way into my world?

"Hi everyone. Alberto recently invited me to photograph the world of Cirque du Palm. Since doing so, I've become fond of and inspired by all that is circus. Then, suddenly a vision for the youth's spring show came to me. An edgy theme with ultra-relevance for today's youth."

"Got my attention." Simon dropped his fistful of popcorn into his paper bowl.

"I combined my photographs of the kids in their classes with some computer art images. The result will help you visualize and imagine possibilities for backgrounds, props, and costumes, as well as promotional artwork for posters, table toppers, and circus programs. I put a lot of work into this. I wanted my idea come alive for you all."

"We're on a budget." Milly pointed her pen at Thomasina.

"Milly, please." Alberto patted the air with his palm. "Thomasina, I'm interested in everyone seeing your ideas. But first, introduce and give an elevator pitch of your idea. The one you gave me the other day."

Behind my back. Pre-mediated. She kept her idea and pictures all to herself.

"Certainly, Alberto." Thomasina tapped her keyboard. "There you go. Everyone. I just sent you each of an email attachment with the title, subtitle, short paragraph teaser, and thirteen visuals. You can review it later. For now, just look to the wall and follow along."

Everyone swiveled in their chairs to face the wall.

"My working title for the student's spring show is, *Circus in Dystopia. A Thrilling Adventure.*"

I nearly fell out of my chair.

"*Circus in Dystopia* is a story about a sixteen-year-old girl named, Bailey. She competes with other kids in a circus arena battleground in hopes to escape her poverty-stricken lifestyle."

Everyone studied the elaborate image.

I grabbed Thomasina's arm and whispered, "Why are you doing this?" I let go. "Why?"

She carried on, unwavering. "Bailey's determined to be chosen as the circus's next ring mistress. All circus performers selected are guaranteed safety and privileges otherwise un-heard of in her dangerous and desolate town. Only one per-former stands in Bailey's way. Her older brother."

"I love it." Alberto clapped.

The guys and Gina and Suki joined in.

"You stole my idea." This time, I grabbed Thomasina's arm and pulled her toward me.

"Ow." She pulled away. "I don't know what you're bloody talking about. Don't embarrass yourself."

"Girl fight. Yeah." Troy and Simon bumped fists.

"Ladies?" Alberto interrupted. "What's going on?"

"Alberto. I'm afraid Thomasina stole my —"

"Everything's fine." She kicked me hard under the table.

"Ow. You —"

"Don't worry, Alberto." Thomasina scooted her chair a few inches away from me. "You know Valthea. You and I talked about it. She's an overachiever who gets emotional."

"No. You've got it all wrong." I felt nauseous. Broken. Furious.

Alberto spoke calmly. "Valthea, listen. I'm ecstatic how well your rehearsals are progressing. The fine-tuning of your act's way ahead of schedule. I want it to stay that way. I don't want you to overextend. You're one of my circus stars. I don't need you to think of a theme. It's okay. I'm so proud to have you in our show." He took a breath. "All right, Thomasina. Back to you."

I raised my arm, as if in school. "Excuse me, Alberto. I promise you. The idea Thomasina's presenting isn't her idea. It's mine. I call it, *Circtopia*. Please. I'll maintain my training and rehearsals while working on this theme and the student show."

"That's great, Valthea, but Alberto didn't call this meeting for you to promise to do what you've been paid to do. Don't be one of those egocentric entertainers. You're not the only one with good ideas." She whispered, loudly, "Don't embarrass yourself anymore." She smiled. "Alberto, may I continue where I left off before Valthea's outburst?"

"I don't mind interruptions. This is a brainstorming session. Thomasina, please play your visuals. We need to vote. I need to go to another meeting."

She flashed her thirteen visuals, near copies of the ones I'd put together. Only better.

Troy, Simon, Gina and Suki cheered and cooed. Made me sick.

"Lights back on, please." Alberto pointed.

Troy hit the lights.

"Please, Alberto. I've proof that *Circtopia* was my idea." I held the manila envelope holding my pamphlets.

Thomasina snatched it from me and pulled it under the table. "Please, Valthea." She shoved the envelope into her tote bag. "Don't undermine me. You know, I've spent day and night working on this project."

"You mean stealing my work."

Suki whispered to Gina, "Is Valthea jealous?"

Alberto stood. "Ladies. Please resolve your sibling squabble at home. Right now, we need to vote. All those in favor of Thomasina's dystopian Circus theme, raise your hands."

Everyone but Milly and I raised a hand.

"All for the around the world theme?"

Milly shot up her arm.

"Thank you, Milly. Valthea?" he asked. "Which theme do you vote for?"

"Mine." I raised my arm. "*Circtopia.*"

"I like that name." Alberto leaned forward and spoke in a quieter tone. "I'm sorry, Thomasina. I like Valthea's title better."

It was clear. She'd enchanted the widower.

"It's settled," he said. "We'll meet in two weeks for our next brainstorming session."

Milly hustled Alberto out of the meeting room, chattering on about his next appointment.

Simon grabbed his bottle of water. "Hopefully the next meeting will have more than just girls fighting with words." He and Troy grabbed their bowls of popcorn and left.

I shut Thomasina's laptop. "We'll discuss your plagiarism later."

"Bye, Gina. See you, Suki." Thomasina waved. "Your idea was good, but I'm glad you liked mine."

"The dystopia angle's cool," Suki said, carrying her and Gina's folders and waters.

"Thank you. You're so kind. Really." Thomasina sighed. "Now if only my own sister were happy for me." She furrowed her forehead. "Valthea, I'm proud of *you*. Can't you for once be proud of me?"

Gina and Suki exited without saying goodbye to me.

This had to stop. *She* had to stop.

Fourteen

"Guess I'll have to lunch with Romeo. Alberto's busy." Thomasina slid her laptop into her tote bag.

"Good." I stood at the door. "Then you can tell Romeo the stunt you just pulled. More impactful that way. After all, sinful confessions engage listeners more than tattletales. *Bon apetit.*" I walked out.

"Wait." She followed me to the parking lot.

"I don't want hear it." I quickened my pace. "Until you tell Alberto the truth, I don't want to talk to you. Maybe then I can forgive you. I don't know."

"Valthea, I've nothing to confess. You're missing the point."

"No, you are." I opened my car door, tossed my purse on the driver's seat, and whipped around. "At what *point* did you think it was okay to betray me? Was it when I accepted you into my home, opened you a bank account, or hired an agent to find you a condo? Maybe it was when I gave Dad money to find you a car. Or, when I introduced you to my boss, Alberto, so you could photograph rehearsals or a show. Perhaps, it was when I introduced you to Romeo Bach. I thought you connected with him. Now I realize, you'll simply disappoint him. So, yeah. Tell me. At what point did I miss *your* point?"

She wore her indignant face. "We're twins. That's my point. It's medically proven we act and think alike."

"No, Thomasina. I don't think or act anything like you."

"Yes, you do. Besides, we're of the generation who likes dystopian books and movies. It's natural we both thought of a story along those lines." She sniffled. "I'm so hurt."

"Please."

"Why won't you honor our connection? We're twins. Admit it. We're telepathically connected." She wiped her dry eyes and face as if they were drenched with tears.

My sister wove strands of false silk into her web, nimble as a spider, never entangling herself. "Step back. I'm leaving." I slid into the driver's seat and shut my door.

She tapped on my window.

I lowered it halfway. "Go have lunch with Romeo."

"Things changed. He texted me. We're meeting for dinner instead."

"Whatever. I don't care."

"Wait." She pressed her hands to the glass. "You need to know I love you. I've no hard feelings about your reaction to my succeeding or your denying our telepathic bond."

"Your ability to spin things your way must've taken years to perfect. It's sheer mastery. Truly. Profound."

"There you go again. Overreacting and dramatizing. Like always, I must be the one to take the high road. Fine," she huffed. "I'll let you collaborate with me on developing my show idea. We'll use your title, since Alberto liked it better. See? I'm generous."

"A, I'm not a drama queen. B, Alberto liked my title and my idea. C, you only want to collaborate because you don't know anything about circus."

Sorin slammed the front door. "Where's Thomasina?" His keys clanked louder than usual on the key tray on our foyer table.

I lay on the couch in the living room, under one of the many afghans Auntie Sylvie crocheted. "She's with—"

"At Dad's?" He stood at the foot of the couch.

"No. Dinner with Romeo. She won't be home until later. Why?"

"I need to talk to her."

"Yeah, well, she needs to talk to me."

"About what? Why are you in your pajamas? It's only six-thirty."

"Bad day. Tell you later. Why do you need to talk to Thomasina? What's going on?"

"A lot." He took off his shoes. "You know, for a second, I thought your sister was on my side. Thought she believed in my medical future, my aura or whatever, and showed it by rewriting my letter for Dr. Xiong. Boy, was I fooled." He joined me on the couch, lounging back. He rested his socked-feet on the coffee table. "I should've stuck with my gut feeling. That girl's a conniving trouble maker."

"I won't argue with that." I sat up. "What happened?"

Sorin's phone rang. He checked the screen. "Hold on. It's Dad. Yeah, Dad. What's up?"

My cell rang. "Hi, Aaron."

"Evening, Mrs. Dobra. Your pizza's here. Should I send the young man up?"

"Yes, please. And Aaron, I ordered one for you, too. Hope you like it."

"Thank you so much. You didn't have to do that."

"We appreciate you. Enjoy."

"Thank you, Mrs. Dobra."

I hung up and then checked for any missed phone messages or texts. No apology from Thomasina.

"Dad, wait. Slow down. I can't understand what you're saying. Just park and come up." Sorin set his phone on the coffee table and jogged to the front door. "Dad's coming over. He's upset about something." He unlocked the front door and left it open.

"Sorin, you have any cash for a tip? The pizza guy is on his way up."

"Yeah. Great. I'm starving." He reached into his pocket.

"Excuse me, sir." A young man in a baseball cap stood at our door "I've an extra-large pizza for Dobra."

"Yup, thanks. Here you go."

I didn't get up, go to the kitchen, or help. I couldn't move. The day's emotional drain depleted me.

Sorin brought the pizza, some paper plates, and a roll of paper towels into the living room. He set them on the coffee table. "Wow, it's hot." He headed back to the kitchen. "Drink?"

"That natural root beer sounds good. Thanks."

I opened the pizza box. The aroma of Tuscany swirled around me. Fresh basil. Roasted red pepper. Goat cheese.

The front door slammed.

I leaned forward. "Hi Dad. Come on. Fresh pizza."

He stormed into the living room, tearing out of his windbreaker.

"Dad," Sorin yelled from the kitchen. "What do you want to drink?"

"Anything." He scooted a chair closer to the coffee table and sat. "Where's your sister?"

"At dinner with Romeo. Why?"

Sorin set three chilled mugs of root beer on the coffee table.

"She lied to me. Lied. Do you believe it?"

"She lied to me, too. And not a white lie. A tar-black, sticky lie."

"Really?" Dad brushed his hair back. His eyes burned like a madman. "After we bless this food, we must pray for Romeo's safety."

"Definitely." Sorin sat next to me. "After today, I could just kill Thomasina?"

"Son. Don't say such things. What've you got against Thomasina?"

"Wait. I thought you were mad at her, too. You want us to pray for Romeo's safety?"

"Yes, because if Thomasina thinks of Romeo as a friend, she may try to fix him up. Which would be a disaster. Her matchmaking skills are horrible. We need to pray for Romeo's protection. Keep her from putting him on a dating site." Dad drank half his root beer. "One of my daughters has no common sense. She can't read people. Seeing colors doesn't help her."

"Then who are you mad at?" I set my mug on the table. "Who lied?"

"Colleen." Dad stood. "I'm crazy furious. My heart's breaking into a million pieces. I can't eat. But—" He sat. "I'm an emotional eater. I'll devour this entire pizza in five minutes. Let's order another one."

"Really?" Sorin asked.

"No. Never mind. Let's pray." Dad bowed his head. "Dear God, please bless this food we are about to eat. Please protect Romeo from Thomasina's lousy matchmaking. And please help me forget about Colleen, and never let me fall in love again. Amen."

"Amen." Sorin took a piece of pizza. "Wow, Dad. What happened?"

"Colleen's a kind and lovely woman. What did she lie about?" I couldn't eat. "And I can't say amen to you never falling in love again."

"I'm sorry, Val. Colleen's not as she seems. She lied about several things." He pushed up his sleeves and grabbed a paper plate. "We all thought she was kind and lovely. And sweet. Wonderful. Perfect."

"Dad. How do you know that Colleen lied?"

"Thomasina told me."

"Shocker," Sorin muttered.

Spider Girl. Of course. "Go on."

Dad shook his head. "Thank goodness, your sister searched Colleen online. She googled her name, went through her Facebook page. Called me immediately with the terrible news. Poor girl blames herself for the whole mess." Dad scooped a piece of pizza out of the box. A web of cheese strands stretched from the box to his palm.

I wanted to sever the strands. I handed him a plastic knife and a paper towel.

"Thanks."

"What'd Colleen lie about?" Sorin asked, between chews.

"Lot of things." Dad crumpled the paper towel in his fist. "Her age. She's two years older than she told me. She dyes her hair that reddish-blonde color. She hates the taste of lamb yet ate a gyro with me when we went to a Greek restaurant. Her real name isn't Colleen. It's Eunice. She has three cats, not one. For fun, one night at the beach, I taught her the basics of how to do a handstand. Turns out, she doesn't like to be upside down." He blotted his eyes with the paper towel. "Lies. All lies." He took a huge bite of his pizza.

"What did she say when you asked about it?" Sorin put another piece of pizza on his plate. "It's not like she lied about anything major or shocking. I thought you were going to tell us she was a foreign spy or married to a mafia hitman. And three cats instead of one, who cares?" He bit into his pizza. "What's her real hair color?"

"Sorin."

"Just asking."

Men.

"I didn't ask her why she lied. I left her a message this afternoon, breaking our dinner date for tonight. I broke up with her."

Sorin stopped chewing. "You left her a message? What are you, fourteen?"

"Dad, seriously, you broke up over hair color? Women don't share that stuff until later. As far as the gyro and handstand, sometimes women like trying new things and adventures to please the man she cares about. She's old school. She's into you."

"How do you know? You saw a past vision?"

"No, Dad. I observed and listened. Colleen's in love with you. She'd probably join you in eating a fried insect sandwich rather than miss an opportunity to be with you."

His eyes turned glassy. "But why lie?" He hopped out of his chair and paced. "To trap me?"

"Nah. Val's right. She loves you."

"Dad, she doesn't need to entrap you. You're already enchanted. And you loved it." I picked up my phone. "If you don't call Colleen and talk this through, I'm calling her."

"Go ahead." He threw his arms in the air. "She's dead to me."

"Don't say that." I wanted to cry.

"That's it." Sorin threw down his pizza crust on his plate and stood. "You can't be that way anymore. You don't even know or care how many people you hurt with your stubbornness. I know you're a big-hearted, loving guy, but sometimes you take your grievances too far. It hurts people. It hurt me."

"Son, what are you talking about?"

"When I was sixteen, I told you I wanted to go to med school and not take over the troupe. You wouldn't listen to anything I had to say. You gave me the silent treatment. Do you even remember that winter? After ten days, I wrote you a ten-page letter. After five days, you read it. You asked me to go for a short walk. It lasted nearly an hour. But you listened to everything I needed to say. You finally lightened up on your bullheadedness and said okay."

"I'm sorry, Son. I never meant to—thank you for telling me. I needed to hear that."

"It's all right. The past is the past. You and I are great. But you need to call Colleen."

"I will. I love you both." Dad grabbed his cell phone and his jacket. "Thanks for the pizza. I'll call her from home."

C.K. Mallick

"Good."

"Night, Dad."

He closed the door behind him.

"Hey, Val. How'd your meeting go? Sorry, I didn't call this afternoon. I got caught up."

"Me, too. In my sister's web. What happened with you?"

He huffed. "Same thing."

"Figured. You go first."

Sorin sat back. "At five o'clock, Dr. Xiong announced who'd be his new assistant."

"But that's the good part, right? He picked you."

"Wrong. Thomasina ruined that with her basket of English biscuits. She visited the main office at my school today. She asked about the Tai-chi classes offered on Saturdays and then chatted with one of the secretaries. One of the older ones, who loves me, told me later that Thomasina rambled on about how I really wanted to be a traditional doctor, but settled for Acupuncture. Not cool. She said, Thomasina knew Dr. Xiong was around the corner listening. What he heard, made him change his mind about me being his assistant."

"Oh no."

"Oh yeah. He's an excellent acupuncturist with an amazing past. I wanted to be close to him and learn and absorb everything."

"I'm so sorry, Sorin. I know you were psyched." Blasted Thomasina. I was furious at her, but also wondered. Did Sorin feel he was settling? Maybe he needed to realize how much he loved alternative medicine and acupuncture.

"Now I'll be less than a regular student to Dr. Xiong."

"Then tell him the truth. Your sister-in-law just moved here and doesn't know you. Write a letter stating how excited you are about acupuncture. Speak from heart. Be passionate."

"Brilliant." He put his arm around me. "I like it. That's exactly what I'm going to do."

"Taking the time to do so will convince any part of you still holding onto the glamour of traditional medicine."

"You're right. Thanks, Val. You know me well. Now, let's hear about you. Before you tell me about your sister's shenanigans, give me the good news. Go ahead. Brag. Did you blow away Alberto with *Circtopia*? He loved it, didn't he?"

"Yeah." I felt sick. "He loved it."

Fifteen

Dad and I met at the costume storage room at three pm, after rehearsal at the big top. Alberto insisted we borrow whatever costume we liked for that evening's, Cirque du Palm Valentine, masquerade ball. The ones we ordered online never arrived.

"I'm excited for tonight, but nothing like the last minute to stress a girl out." I unlocked the door.

"I don't understand it." Dad pushed the door open. "Thomasina's had hers over a week."

"What is it?"

"Won't tell me. Smells good in here, not musky or like mothballs."

I flipped on the lights. The crowded room, the size of a small boutique, held hundreds of sparkly costumes, categorized in rows, hanging on racks, and from bars suspended from ceiling chains.

"Ha! Look at this place. Rosa would love it."

"Take some pictures and send them to her."

"Good idea." Dad snapped a few photos with his cell phone. "Maybe they'll entice her and Bruno to visit soon."

Dad's older sister, Rosa, designed costumes for The Gypsy Royales. She and Bruno held a dear place in my heart. They were the only troupe members, besides Dad and Sorin, to welcome me, a sixteen-year-old outsider, in the troupe for their summer tour.

We set our phones and keys on a file cabinet next to a fragrance diffuser with black reeds. The label read, Lime Basil and Mandarin. "No wonder it smells good in here."

"Which way first?"

"Left." I pointed. "The other side has the trapeze costumes and their massive capes."

"No thong for me, thank you very much."

"Dad, they wear tights."

He led us to the first row, stopping halfway. He pushed several flamenco dresses to the side, making room for a black and silver, bull-fighting costume. "What do you think, Val?"

"Maybe. The hat's kind of goofy. Should we dress in the same theme?" I held out one of the flamenco costume's black-and-red ruffle skirt. "I can't believe Thomasina texted you this morning, saying she won't come to the ball unless I apologize to her. Absurd." I walked to the next row.

"Val, why don't you apologize? You pushed her away. I don't understand why you can't accept the fact that you girls think alike sometimes. You're twins. It is possible to come up with the same idea. I read a story online about twin girls who painted nearly the same painting, yet they lived in two different countries."

"Maybe, but that isn't the case here. I'm telling you, she stole my idea. Thomasina presented my idea down to every detail at that staff meeting. No, Dad. I won't apologize for her blatant plagiarism or her refusal to take responsibility for her behavior. Any counselor will tell you, manipulation is a way of life for someone with a Personality Disorder."

"I can't believe you assume all these negative things about your sister. You and Sorin even blame her of sabotaging my relationship with Colleen."

Dad didn't get it, and I didn't have three hours to explain how his youngest daughter operated. I held out my hand, feeling the kitten-soft plumes of costumes in turquoise, orange, and fuchsia. "Is Colleen coming to the ball?"

"I pray so."

"I thought you were mad at her. Sheesh. You're as confusing as Thomasina." Both he and Thomasina were dramatic, but Dad was sane and his intention well-meaning. Plus, Dad had a warm heart. Thomasina had no—"

"I thought about what you and Sorin said the other night. So, I called her. But she won't answer. I know, last night she was with her church group at a soup kitchen. But what about today? I left her five messages telling her I wanted to meet in person and listen to her."

His expression, tone, and body language made it clear. He was in love with her. "Good, Dad. I'm proud of you. She'll call you back when she's ready. Maybe she'll come to the ball."

"She must, or I'll go crazy." Dad pointed to costumes in front of me. "What about that?"

"This one?" I pushed aside the women's costumes.

"Yeah."

I pulled out the hanger holding the black, Zorro ensemble. A sword and a silk scarf with eyeholes hung from the hanger. "This year's theme is, Lovers: Famous and Unknown. Who did Zorro love?"

He took the costume. "Whoever Colleen dresses like tonight." He checked the shirt collar. "My size. Zorro, it is. I'm signing out this one." He carried it over his shoulder.

"Now we need something for me and Sorin."

"You got to admit, I'm kind of like Zorro already."

"How do you figure?" I stopped to check out a Samurai warrior costume and a geisha gown. "I wear black. I care about those in need. I'm dashing. Hey, you and Sorin would make a great Cleopatra and Marc Anthony."

"Thanks, Dad, but it's a common choice. Negative story-end." I kept us moving further down the aisle.

"How about something with flourish?" Dad stopped at a group of Louis IVX-style costumes. "Like these."

Wigs sat displayed on the shelf above the men's waistcoats and pantaloon breeches and above the women's powder-blue and gold gowns. "Val, you dress as Marie Antoinette and Sorin—"

"Dad."

"That's right. Sorry. Forgot about that." He drew one hand across his throat, making a gurgle sound.

"Nice sound effects." I curved around to the next row. "There has to be something Sorin and I can wear."

"Here you go. You love this whole King Arthur, Medieval time."

"Yes, I do." I pressed back an exquisite red gown, trimmed in brocade and dotted with crystals. "This is perfect for Guinevere. I do love the ideals of Camelot."

"Plus, you already call Sorin your champion."

"Except my champion's still mad at me for tolerating Thomasina. He wants me to sit down with Alberto and show him the dated documentation of my idea." I hung the gown. "He thinks I'm bending my principals to compensate for time lost."

"He thinks you're trying to catch up and be the best sister in the world?"

"Yeah. At least Sorin is coming tonight."

"Even if my son's upset, he remains loyal and supportive."

"He's the best."

"Come on, Valthea. Focus and pick two costumes. I need to shower and shave. Spruce up. Be ready for Colleen."

I continued to sort through costumes. "I need to find the perfect—"

"Not those, Val. They're peasant's clothes with sequins."

"What about these? Robin Hood and Maid Marion from Sherwood Forest meets Las Vegas." I held up the fern-green and amber costumes and their bow and sheath of arrows. Robin's ensemble included tunic, tights, and boots decorated with sequins and studs. Marion's included fishnet stockings, hot pants, boots, and a corset, sewn chockful of rhinestones.

"Ha! It's perfect. Like Zorro, you two rob from the rich and give to the poor." He took the costumes from my arms. "I'll carry these. Can you sign us out?"

"Sure. Thanks."

"Val, I don't know if I told you how proud I am of you."

"Thanks, Dad. You tell me all the time, but I appreciate it every time."

"I'm talking about when you inherited that money from your mom and Sylvie. First thing you did was give to those two orphanages in Bucharest. You're truly Gisella's daughter."

"It's something I always wanted to do, and Dad, I'm *your* daughter, too." I wrote our names and the costume's tag number on the sign-out clipboard. "I'm proud of Sorin. He's the one who thought of stocking the orphanages with some medical supplies."

"You both have hearts without borders. Now all you have to do is forgive your sister."

Three hours later, Sorin yelled from the living room. "Are you ready? Dad's here."

"Be right there," I yelled. I rotated in front of our bedroom mirror one more time. Long red wig and black thigh-high boots. He'll love it. Tight corset, hot pants and fishnet tights. He'll die. I smiled, quickly slinging on my bow and arrows and grabbing my shoulder bag. I slowed to enter the living room. "Marion is now ready."

Sorin froze, ga-ga eyed.

Dad threw his arms wide. "Where's my teen daughter?"

"Dad, I'm grown up, a professional entertainer, and a married woman. Sorin, how do you like my costume?" I bat my eyes. I'd glued on two rows of false lashes. "Am I a dangerous beauty?"

"Sure." He chugged a water.

That's it? I wanted Sorin to go on about my sexy gorgeousness. Water, over these hot pants? Forget it. I vowed never again to ask him for a compliment. I held my head high. "You gentlemen look handsome tonight."

"Thank you, but we can't compete with you." Dad rammed Sorin's shoulder with his. "Your wife looks stunning, doesn't she?"

Mute husband.

Was Sorin bored of my appearance, holding a grudge, or restraining what he really felt? Juvenile. "Thank you for the compliment, Dad."

Sorin slung his bow on one shoulder. "You look good."

Good? I wasn't a terrier.

"Ready, kids?" Dad opened the front door.

I took my time walking past Sorin.

He whispered, "You look hot."

I melted with relief. Arguing with your soul mate bleeds your heart. I felt like running to him, hugging him tight, and kissing him all over. If I did that, he'd learn breadcrumbs thrown at my feet were sufficient, all I was worth. They weren't. I winked and walked past him.

He nearly fell over himself locking the door behind us.

The art of the chase. It mustn't stop after the wedding.

We walked toward the elevator. Zorro, Maid Marion, and Robin Hood. We approached Dad's condo.

"Dad, let's knock. Maybe Thomasina wants to come with us."

"Don't bother." Dad kept me and Sorin moving. "I tried for an hour. She won't answer or come out."

"He's right, Val. She's a big girl. She can drive herself if she decides to come."

I glanced over my shoulder. Dad's door cracked open, exposing a glimmer of something sparkly before it closed.

Sorin pressed the elevator's down arrow.

Thomasina's ego was too grand to miss the chance to attend a ball.

One of our cell phones rang as we exited the elevator.

"That's yours, Val."

I pulled my phone from my purse. "Hi Grama, how are you?"

"A little tired. What about you, dear?"

"Val, tell your grandmother, Dad and I say hi. We'll go get the car." Sorin and Dad headed to the Maserati, parked five rows away.

"Grama, Sorin and Dad say hi. We're on our way to the masquerade ball tonight."

"That's right. How exciting. Thomasina with you?"

"Uh, she's coming later."

"Everyone getting along?"

"To be honest, it's been challenging. Grama, my family and situations are collapsing around me. I don't know what to do. Thomasina's—"

"A black streak?"

"Streak or sheep, yeah."

"Valthea, you've common sense and you're insightful. You must restore your family and your life one person at a time. Speak up. Be honest. Don't make the same mistakes I did in the past. Perhaps, start with your sister. Shoot straight with her about what you're feeling.

"But she's the instigator of the entire mess. Everything was fine before she came."

"Dear, you can't blame life's ripples on your sister."

Dad pulled up in his freshly waxed and detailed sportscar. Sorin hopped out from the backseat and held open the front passenger door.

"Thanks, Grama. I got to go. I'll try your idea. I'll call you tomorrow afternoon after dress rehearsal."

"My goodness. You've a dress rehearsal the morning after the ball?"

"Weird timing, I know. Maybe Alberto's testing our discipline."

"In any case, have fun tonight. You deserve it. Do consider reaching out to your sister. After all, once I'm gone, you'll be the new matriarch of the Adamescu family."

"Me? What about Aunt Szusanna? I'm sure she thinks she's going to be queen."

"Doesn't matter what Szusanna thinks or wants. I decide who receives and manages what monies and properties. Never mind all that now. Go have a magnificent time. We'll talk tomorrow. I want to hear all the details, especially how beautiful my granddaughters looked."

"We'll take lots of pictures. Love you, Grama. Talk to you tomorrow. Bye." I put away my phone and stood by the backseat door. "I'm sitting next to you, Robin Hood."

"I like that idea." He quickly shut the front door and opened the back door.

I held my bow side and slid in.

Sorin shut the door and joined me from the other side.

Dad eyeballed us via the rearview mirror. "Guess I'm your chauffeur tonight, kids."

"That's right, Dad."

Dad turned the radio up.

Sorin whispered, "You all right? You look worried." He held my gloved hand in his.

Champions always know. "Sorin, if Grama Alessia makes me the matriarch of the Adamescu's estate, how far do you think Aunt Szusanna will go to ruin my life? She already tried to ruin our wedding."

"What do you say, we talk about this the day after tomorrow?"

"I'd say you were a very wise man, even with that Robin Hood moustache."

He laughed. "Thank you, Maid Marion."

All right. Grama Alessia suggested I shoot straight, one person at a time. I didn't believe in coincidences, but my costume happened to include a bow with *four* arrows. I took a deep breath. Arrow number one: me and Sorin. Thank goodness, we were close again. Bullseye. Arrow number two: Dad. He was back pursuing Colleen. Right on target. Arrow number three: Alberto. Tonight, I'd prove *Circtopia* was mine, shooting an arrow through the air for all to see.

Dad sped around the corner. In minutes, we'd arrive at CDP's arena.

Arrow number four: Thomasina. Now was the time. I pulled out all the poison arrows she'd shot into my heart and flung them out the window. Tonight, I'd tell her. My tolerating her narcissistic behavior was done. I'd then stand firm, draw back the fourth arrow, and fire it straight at her forehead.

Sixteen

The three of us walked the red carpet leading to the entrance of the Cirque du Palm arena. Twisted ivy vines and dark red roses covered the area around its double doors. The awaiting doormen wore classic Venetian carnival costumes. Their white masks with long pointed noses creeped me out. I stepped between Sorin and Dad, looping my arms through theirs.

"Wow, Val, your circus director really knows how to throw a fund-raiser. I can hear the music from out here."

"I can't wait to see what the decorating committee did inside. CDP announced their theme to the press three months ago. They've had plenty of time to work their magic."

"And Son, listen to this. All the ball's performers are advanced students from the school. Some of whom Valthea coaches."

"Dad, you coached some, too."

"Then I'm sure they'll be great."

Crows cawed in the sky above us. They flew toward a group of pine trees behind the circus offices. I gripped Sorin's forearm. "A murder of crows ...."

Sorin looked up, squinting. "Since when are you superstitious?"

"I'm not. They just remind me of ...never mind."

Dad patted my arm. "Val, if you're worried about the full rehearsal tomorrow, don't be. You're ready. Your act's stupendous."

"Thank you both. I'm fine. I just miss Nawa and Aunt Sylvie."

"Ah, Miss Sylvie. God rest her soul." Dad's voice drifted. "She'd be so proud of you. But you have her sister, your Grandmother Alessia. You two got along so well and in no time at all."

C.K. Mallick

"Grama Alessia's easy to be with. Planning the wedding really bonded us."

One of the doormen greeted us. "Welcome to the castle."

"Ha! The castle." Dad cupped his palm on the top of his sword. "Staying in character, eh, guys? Keeping the fantasy going?"

The other doorman took our tickets. He scanned them with a handheld device and then typed in our names.

The first doorman stepped forward. "Are you ready for the night of your life?"

"Absolutely." Dad shot his arms overhead, playing up his Zorro self.

"Don't get my dad started."

"Sorin." I nudged him. "I mean, Robin Hood. Let Dad play."

He grinned. "Okay, Maid Marion."

I turned around, grabbed him by his tunic, and pulled him in close. "It's Marion. No maid. Just Marion." I let him go and faced the doors. He needed a moment for his pulse to rise and his mind to harden with interesting thoughts. Of me.

"Hustle, you two." Dad rubbed his hands together. "I'm ready for the night of my life. Remember, text me if you spot Colleen."

"We will."

"Dad, why don't you call her now?"

"I tried a couple of minutes ago. Something's wrong with her service."

"She probably threw her phone in the middle of the highway when you wouldn't listen to her."

"I wouldn't blame her.

The doormen opened the doors a few inches. We glimpsed the low-lit castle interior and the sound of Beethoven's fifth mixed with a techno beat. I caught a whiff of a heady scent.

"What's that smell?" Dad sniffed the air. "Perfume?"

The first doorman answered. "Black rose and sandalwood. The castle's choice."

"It's heavy."

"No, Sorin, it's mysterious."

"Guests, please listen." The second doorman spoke more affected than before. "After you enter, you climb four steps to a platform. Pause there. Allow the guests inside to see you."

"Good idea. Kids, make sure we pause long enough for Colleen to spot us."

"Sir, I'm afraid you must descend the four steps when the music changes. Others are waiting their turn. Two footmen will welcome you at the base of the platform."

"Carpe noctem." The doormen said in sync and opened the doors wide.

Red lighting and the scent of rose and sandalwood hit us all at once. It set a mood of intrigue and sensuality.

We climbed the steps, edged in glow-tape, to the dark entrance platform. The arena thumped with classical music mixed with techno.

"Ha! Now this is a party." Cosmo bowed to the crowd below.

"It's awesome," Sorin said.

"I can't believe it's the same arena. It's beautiful." I beamed as she scanned the venue.

Hundreds of costumed guests danced, laughed, ate and drank. Banners with heart-shaped crests hung high from the ceiling. A team of flying trapeze artists swung and somersaulted through the air on one side of the arena. On the other, high-wire artists held balancing poles and walked in a human pyramid across their wire—thirty feet in the air. Fire breathers, speed jugglers, and hand balancers performed on pillar platforms. Clowns worked the floor with gags and skits and interacted with the guests. A trio of silk aerialists wrapped, unrolled, and posed on the red silks hanging above the center of the dance floor.

"You two are part of an amazing organization."

"Val and I love it. Cirque's topnotch."

The techno version of Beethoven's Fifth Symphony ricocheting around us, cut to the Andrew Lloyd Webber's, The Phantom of the Opera overture. The striking score enveloped me like a black opera cape. Alberto chose the opera's piece, Music of the Night for my Roman Rings act. I took it as a good sign for tomorrow.

The spotlight hit us. The proverbial black opera cape flew open. The guests on the dance floor applauded and cheered.

Dad waved to the crowd, forever a showman. "I love this."

Sorin shielded his eyes. "I can't see." He stepped forward, ready to walk down the platform's steps.

"Please wait, sir," said one of the footmen.

He backed up in line with Dad.

The pair of capped footmen wore black turtlenecks and tights, their torso sandwiched between jumbo playing cards. One the Jack of Spades, the other the Jack of Hearts.

"Val. Sorin. Check it out." Dad drew his sword and pointed the tip at the digital sign, five feet above our heads. "That was my idea."

A sign lit up, scrolling out our names like a stock market ticker.

"Very clever, Dad." Sorin patted him on the back. "A modern version of trumpets sounding and announcing guests arrival."

"Thanks, Son. If Colleen or Thomasina are here, they'll now know we are, too."

The spotlight shut off. The overture gave way to a jacked up, dance version of Vivaldi's concerto, Summer. We stood blinded on the dark platform. The footmen directed their flashlights to the steps.

I held Sorin's arm, and we descended the platform into the action.

Dad pulled us to the side. "I need a second to get my night eyes. Then I'll scope the place for Colleen."

"Dad, relax. We were just lit up for all to see, including her."

"What if she was in the powder room?" He tore off his scarf mask. "This thing's driving me crazy.

"You have to wear a mask. It's a masquerade ball." I stepped behind him. "Give it to me. You probably tied it too tight."

"Sorin, you have your phone on vibrate, right? Val, you too."

"Yeah, Dad. We triple checked our phones in the car, remember?"

I finished tying Dad's scarf mask. "There you go. Devilishly handsome. A true Zorro. Ready for Colleen."

"Thanks. It feels better. Val, do you think your sister will show tonight?"

"She'll be here."

"You sound confident." Sorin tugged on his Robin Hood jacket. "Personally, I hope she does show."

I couldn't believe it. There was hope for this night yet.

A security man escorted out a drunken, sixty-year-old woman dressed like a Barbie doll. A tan, wrinkled man, dressed in army fatigues followed.

"G.I. Joe?"

"I guess. You know your toys, Sorin."

"This party's intoxicating," Dad yelled over the music. "I feel high, yet I haven't had a sip to drink."

The Phantom of the Opera overture blasted from the speakers.

"Same music? Who's the DJ?"

"Sorin." Dad pointed to the entrance platform. "They play that piece every time someone new enters. That way, we know it's time to stare and applaud. Like people did we walked in."

"The DJ's training us like Pavlov's dog."

"Exactly."

A couple dressed as Gomez and Mortica Addams stood on the platform. The digital sign read, Dr. & Mrs. Nagamori.

"Kids, I'm off, hunting for Colleen."

"Okay. Good luck, Dad."

Dad pivoted away, sharp as a tango dancer.

"Babe," Sorin said. "Although you are no doubt the most delicious morsel here. Let's get some food. I'm starving."

"Well, since you put it that way —"

"But first, come here for a second." Sorin drew me away from the crowd and behind a mock Roman pillar. We kissed until our masks hit.

"Hold on." I took off my mask. "I love your affection, but maybe we should —"

"Take off more than our masks?" He slid his mask from his eyes to his head as smooth as he did his Ray Ban's.

"Are you proposing a rendezvous in our bedroom later tonight?"

"Definitely. A rendezvous where I remove your costume, piece-by-piece. I can't wait to experience you as a redhead."

"And I can't wait to experience you with that moustache."

I slowed my breathing, hoping it'd calm my arousal. It didn't.

A tuxedoed server presented his tray. "Spicy crab cakes?"

"Absolutely." Sorin placed four on a napkin. "Thanks."

"Now that you have a bit of food, let's check out some of the performers."

"Sure." He popped a crab cake in his mouth.

We watched the silk aerialists perform and then the speed juggler. We joined a small crowd gathering to watch the clown dressed as a dentist.

We cheered and applauded at the end of the clown's hysterical, five-minute schtick using a giant toothbrush and ten sets of supersized clapping teeth. Sorin and I applauded. The man next to us whistled like he was at a rock concert. He stood out in head to toe purple, resembling the music icon, Prince. Next to him stood an athletic, Latin-looking woman in a white midriff-top and a pair of white bellbottoms. Instead of clapping, she raised one arm overhead and twirled a blond wood drumstick between her fingers. She did so with the fluidity of a pro. She held a white-lace mask to her eyes with her other hand. I took a double-take. The stick attached to her mask was also a blond wood drumstick.

The crowd broke away, and we continued exploring the castle. "Val." Sorin pointed. "What's at that table?"

A dozen women crowded around an eight-foot-long table with goblets, cylinder vases, and fishbowls, filled with red, black, white, and pink candy.

"It's called a candy *bar*."

"How ironic. We're going from a dentist clown to a candy bar. Come on, let's see if there's any gummy bears." Sorin took my hand, and we squeezed our way to the front of the table. Licorice sticks, chocolate kisses, bubble gum cigars, heart-shaped mints with messages, and gummy bears. The women around us chattered and giggled. Sorin scooped a cup of gummy bears. "Let's leave the addicts to their fix."

I spotted Alberto and Milly about twenty feet away. "I'll be right back. I need to talk to Alberto for a minute."

"Are you showing him the proof?"

"Yes." Arrow number three.

"Good. I'm glad. I'll be at the pasta bar, *Marion*."

"All right, *Hood*." I headed toward Alberto, sliding past a Bonnie and Clyde couple. They held authentic-looking toy, machine guns. Kind of disturbing.

A man and a woman wearing black tights and leotards with wings, toasted flutes of champagne.

I had to stop. "Excuse me. Hi. Just curious. What are you two supposed to be?"

"Lovebugs."

"Neat." What else could I say?

"Valthea?"

"Alberto."

He waved me over. Alberto dressed as the phantom, from The Phantom of the Opera. He wore his formal tux, opera cape, and white, half mask to perfection.

Milly stood next to him, wearing a white halter dress, gold arm bands, and a Cleopatra wig.

"Good evening, Alberto. Milly. It's an incredible party, I mean ball." I didn't know whether to speak to Alberto's eye behind his phantom's half mask, or his exposed eye. I glanced at the swarms of guests filling the arena. "You and the committee thought of everything."

"They did an outstanding job. I'm glad you like it."

"Your costume choice is perfect, Alberto. You look regal and handsome. You look wonderful, too, Milly."

"Thank you, Valthea. I've always identified with Cleopatra. She was a brilliant strategist, as well as seductress."

"Uh, right. Excuse me, Milly, do you mind if I talk to Alberto a moment?"

"You may. I need to go check on my candy bar. Have you seen it? I choose each delectable myself."

"Good job. The table's packed."

"No surprise." Milly headed toward her candy bar.

"Are you enjoying yourself, Valthea?"

"Yes, sir. Sorin, Dad, and I love the whole thing. The set up. The mystique. It's grand."

"Wonderful. Wonderful. So, what's on your mind? Need to talk about the student show?"

"Yes, sir. I do."

"I'm glad."

"You are?" I pulled my cell phone from my shoulder bag.

"Yes. Go on."

"Okay. Alberto, I just need to set the record straight. I'll let it go after that, and you can get back to your guests." I increased the brightness of my cell phone screen.

"Hold on. Let me put on some glasses." Alberto slid his mask to the top of his head and put on a pair of readers.

I handed him my phone. "Scroll down and note the dates on this series of emails I sent myself."

"Uh, huh." He used his index finger to scroll. "I see."

"It's all there. My concept for *Circtopia*. The show's outline. My ideas for *Circtopia's* costumes, props, and marketing ideas. Everything. Exactly like the ones—"

"Like the ones Thomasina presented at the meeting. Yes, I see." He returned my phone.

I turned it off and stuffed it in my purse.

"Valthea, I apologize. Your sister's pitch was very convincing. I fell for it, and for a moment, her."

"It's okay, Sir. In one way or another, we all did."

"So, all she thought of was a different show title."

"Yes, sir. That's correct. The rest was pure plagiarism. After that meeting, Thomasina asked me to assist her. She doesn't know anything about circus or show biz. Alberto, just so you know, circus is everything to me. I want to grow with it, choreograph, create, and maybe eventually direct. I don't know what Thomasina wants, or why she lied. Sibling rivalry. Keep Romeo's attention. Whatever the case, you now know the truth."

"Thank you for coming and talking to me. I understand the sibling rivalry thing. I'm from a family of four boys. After I reviewed how the meeting went that day, I suspected you the real creator of *Circtopia*. I analyzed what you two said, whispered, and your body language."

"You *read* people?"

"Have to." He shrugged. "I'm in the entertainment business. Mouths lie, bodies don't. That night, Romeo called me. Wanted to talk to me about a few things, including what he'd heard happened in the meeting. He told me you shared your idea with him a week prior."

Thank you, Romeo Bach.

"Come. I'd like a glass of wine." We walked to the wine bar. "Valthea, Romeo's one of those rare individuals who tries to do the right thing. I try to choose my cast and crew for their expertise, but also their integrity and disposition. I prefer a healthy, show biz family, over a toxic one."

The bartender poured Alberto a glass of merlot.

"Val, I'm glad you gave me a second chance to hear the truth and gave yourself a second chance to express the truth."

"Thank you for listening, Sir."

"Part of a director's or choreographer's job is knowing how to work with a performer. Their personality, their dramas. It's also helpful when a performer knows when and how to speak to their director or choreographer. Thank you for your communication, Valthea. You've a healthy spine and a strong backbone. Keep it up. You need both for circus."

"Yes, sir. Thank you."

"We've partial dress rehearsal tomorrow, but on Monday, I'll announce you the real creator of *Circtopia*. The staff will work with you and your ideas."

"I'm ecstatic."

"I wanted Thomasina to confess the truth." He brushed his phantom cape back and sipped his wine. "She needs to work on her backbone."

The Phantom of the Opera overture boomed from nearby speakers. The spotlight lit four people on the entrance platform. Two guys dressed like Felonius Gru and Dru from Despicible Me 3, the animated film. The two others donned capes and masks as Batman and Catwoman.

"Mr. and Mrs. Flanigan, Batman and Catwoman are new investors of CDP."

The DJ cutaway from the opera overture to a disco/Mozart piece. This ended the new arrivals' fifteen seconds of fame.

"Alberto," I said over the music. "Thanks again for listening and believing in me."

"Of course. Now go, Valthea. Enjoy your evening We've a big day tomorrow."

"We do. Thanks. I'll go find my husband."

Two pirates greeted Alberto. I spotted Sorin standing by the hot-appetizer table.

"Sorin —"

"Hey Val." He held out his red, plastic plate filled with food. Try one of the spinach pies."

"No thanks. I'm not hungry yet."

"All good with Alberto? "

"Yes. In fact, I feel light as a feather, even in this wig and these boots."

"Let's sit over there. Away from the crowd. I want to hear about it." Sorin led us to a corner of the arena decorated as a fairy tale garden, lit with strings of white lights. A banner with an old fashion, fairy tale font read, The Romantic Garden.

Red rose bushes and artificial fir trees encircled the area's oval, fleur-de-li print carpet. Three, eight-foot-tall constructed cottage fronts sat propped up. Chunky, pine tree stumps served as end tables for the three red velvet loveseats.

We sat on the middle loveseat. "I told Alberto the truth about my project. Monday, he'll announce that I'm the true creator of *Circtopia*."

Sorin set his plate on the tree stump and wrapped his arms around me. "Proud of you, babe." He kissed my cheek, or rather my wig, before letting me go. "You spoke up against your sister's lie. That's hard."

"Especially when you meet a sister you didn't know existed. Sorin, I know you think I've let Thomasina get away with murder since she's come into our lives."

"I think you've had a high, pain tolerance for her wacky behavior because you don't want to lose her. But Val, if she really loves you, she'll accept some healthy boundaries."

"That's true." I scooted closer to him. "There's another reason I give her so many second chances. What if my mother's dying prayer was for her children and their father to reunite? To be family. No matter the ups or downs."

Sorin put his arm around me.

I rested my head on his shoulder. "I don't want to disappoint my mother."

Seventeen

I stood with Sorin at the table serving Asian cuisine. "Val, isn't that Romeo Bach?" He pointed to several tall men dressed as Musketeers. They had their backs to us.

"I don't think so."

"Romeo!" he called and waved.

A shorter man stepped out from the group. He waved and headed our way. He wore a blue velvet jacket and bellbottom pants, white ruffled shirt, and a pair of black, horn-rimmed glasses. He greeted us with hugs. "You two look great."

"Thanks. We're Robin Hood and Maid, I mean, Marion."

"Romeo," I asked. "Who are you supposed to be?"

"Babe. Come on." Sorin put his arm around me. "He's Austin Powers."

"I saw that movie. Fun choice."

"You mean, dorky choice." Romeo took off his glasses. "I dressed British on purpose for you-know-who. Is she here? I texted her. Left messages. But I haven't heard back."

"We haven't either. Don't worry. Thomasina will show up."

Sorin inched us forward in the line. "Val's positive she's coming tonight."

"I hope so." Romeo checked his phone. "I'd like to talk to her in person. If she comes clean about everything, I'd be willing to give her a second chance. That girl must really be insecure to do the things she's done."

"Insecure is one word for her." Sorin handed me a paper plate filled with noodles, water chestnuts, peapods, and mini corncobs.

"Sorin, this is way too much food."

"Here's one for you, Romeo." Sorin offered him the same. "I'll grab another."

"No thanks, Sorin. You have it." He put his glasses back on. "I need to socialize and network. Please, text me if your sister shows up."

"I will."

"See you."

Sorin found an available high-top table. He attacked his mound of noodles. I nibbled on the mini corn on the cobs.

"Kids!"

"Dad." Sorin scooted around our table.

Dad strutted up to us, holding hands with Miss Colleen. "Look who I found. Ha! My Cinderella."

"Hi, Miss Colleen." We exchanged cheek kisses. "You make a beautiful Cinderella."

"Thank you, Valthea. I love the red hair."

"Thanks."

Sorin hugged Miss Colleen. "We're so glad you're here."

"Thank you, Sorin. I couldn't possibly miss seeing your father dressed as Zorro."

Sorin put his arm around Dad. "Yeah. He looks pretty sharp."

"Sorin, ask Colleen why she dressed as Cinderella. Go on. Ask her."

"Good to see you happy and hyper again, Dad."

"Yeah, yeah. Ask Colleen. Come on." Dad kissed her hand.

"Okay, okay. Miss Colleen. Why did you choose to dress as Cinderella?"

I lifted my mask.

Miss Colleen ...she sat at a bay window, petting a blue-gray cat. "I've lost him, Sherman. Lost him." She kissed the cat's head. "I knew better than to listen to her." Two striped tabbies raced by on the black-and-white tile floor. "But I wanted to meet and fall in love with a wonderful man. And I did." Sherman headbutted her. She pushed him away gently. He headbutted her again. "Sherman!" She picked him up. "Fine. I'll go. I tell him everything."

I got it. Miss Colleen wasn't a liar. She just wanted to get to know Dad before she told him she dyed her hair and her real name was Eunice. It wasn't a big deal until Thomasina spun it into one. She framed Miss Colleen as a liar.

I related. I had fallen in love with the idea of having a sister. I lied to myself, justifying Thomasina's behavior. Sorin headbutted me several times. I didn't listen. Like Miss Colleen, I also fell prey to Thomasina's suggestive promptings.

"I love the story of Cinderella but chose her because of our similarities. I live a fairly isolated life. I love animals and birds. And I wanted to meet and fall in love with a wonderful man." She smiled at Dad. "And I did. Cosmo's my prince."

Dad beamed.

"But," she continued, "like Cinderella, I didn't tell the prince the truth right away. Falling in love can make one foolish at any age."

"Then I've been the most foolish in the world." Dad kissed her cheek.

"Aw, thank you." Miss Colleen kissed him back.

The Phantom of the Opera overture blasted from the speakers, extinguishing a disco mix with Stravinsky's Firebird.

"I'm glad you two are together again." I yelled over the music.

"Me, too. Here." Dad handed Sorin his car keys. "Colleen and I will leave in her carriage tonight."

"You're not leaving now, are you?" He stuffed the keys into his tunic pocket.

"No. We'll stick around for a while."

The spotlight circled the dance floor before landing on the entrance platform.

"My goodness." Colleen lowered her mask. "What a beautiful gown."

"Who's she supposed to be?" Dad pulled down his scarf mask, letting it hang around his neck. "Queen Elizabeth? You know, the first one."

Colleen looped her arm through Dad's. "Or, with that wig, Marie Antoinette. Let's move closer."

Sorin didn't care about costumes. But ever the gentleman, he led us through the crowd until we stood five people away from the platform's steps.

I lifted my mask.

"I know who she's supposed to be," Miss Colleen said. "The Queen of Hearts."

The woman wore an over-the-top, red velvet, ballgown dotted with rhinestones, pearls, and red rosebuds. Her overlaying skirt panels alternated with patterns of hearts and fleur de lis. A heart-shaped pendant the size of an apple lay over her fitted bodice, surrounded by multiple strands of pearls. Her red velvet crown, framed in gold and pearls, rested on her platinum, up-do wig with cascading curls. The woman held her gold scepter as if it were a bouquet of roses she'd won for best costume.

Colleen whispered, "She must've ordered it months ago. Who *is* she?"

"We'll find out in a second." I stared at the digital sign above the platform. "Probably a woman who wants to be queen of the ball."

"Doesn't matter who it is." Dad kissed Miss Colleen with dramatic flourish. "Colleen's the queen of my heart."

The sign lit up. I read aloud. "Thomasina Stratham." Of course.

Dad clapped his hands. "You were right, Val. Your sister came."

My stomach churned. Being right was overrated.

The spotlight closed. Thomasina tossed her handheld eye mask and descended the platform. The DJ played Carmina

Burana. How apropos. Brutal percussion. Pagan sensuality. Chorus in classic Latin. Haunting.

"Thomasina," Dad yelled.

I took a deep breath. Tonight, was the night, I'd speak my mind.

The four of us met her halfway. Thomasina air-hugged Dad. Colleen and I complimented her costume. She said nothing about ours.

"Thomasina, look." Dad put his arm around Colleen. "Isn't it great? I'm back with Colleen. We talked everything out. We understand why you tried to break us up. Thomasina, you never have to worry. You will always be my daughter. I'll always make time for you. All's forgiven."

Colleen lowered her mask. "Let's go forward. The past is in the past. I hold nothing against you."

"What are you people talking about? Daddy, I don't need to be forgiven. I know I'm your daughter forever. Miss Colleen, you, on the flip side, are every man's nightmare."

The veins in Dad's neck bulged. "You need to apologize to Colleen. Right now."

"Thomasina, Miss Colleen and Dad are trying to—"

"Can you two just shush for a second?" Thomasina glared at Miss Colleen. "You lied to my Dad. You're a gold digger and the worst kind. A premeditating strategist. You did your research. Found out what our mother looked like and then tried to copy her appearance. My Dad's smitten with you, but I'm not. You're no better than a high paid—"

"Enough!" Dad stepped in between Thomasina and Miss Colleen.

"It's okay, Cosmo." Colleen placed her hand on his shoulder and stood next to him. "She's just upset."

"No. I'm fabulous. You're upsetting. Daddy, nothing against you. I love you."

"If that's true, don't insult people I care about."

"It's difficult. You care about the wrong people. This is draining. I'm off to socialize and be seen. Toodaloo."

"Miss Colleen, I'm sorry for my sister's behavior. Thomasina's acting, well, extremely Thomasina."

Colleen reached for Dad. "I didn't mean to cause—"

"You did nothing wrong. It's her." Dad kept her in his arms. "Let's go outside. Fresh air helps everything."

"Hey guys." Sorin pointed. "Check out the back of Thomasina's dress."

My eyes couldn't open any wider.

"A therapist could have a field day with that."

Sorin was right.

"The queen of spades," Miss Colleen uttered.

Black, crushed velvet fabric, with streams of black, purple and silver rhinestones, made up the back of Thomasina's ballgown and crown. Stiff black netting, frothed with swirls of glitter, jutted out from her neck collar, waistband, and skirt hem. Black sequin spades, pinstripes, and spider webs trailed down her gown's purple, satin skirt panels.

Sorin took a picture.

"Why'd you take a picture?"

"For Aunt Rosa. She won't believe it."

Thomasina sauntered away, swinging her scepter with every step. She welcomed the attention of every ball attendee who complimented and fawned over her with self-effacing charm.

Spade, indeed.

I took off, following her.

"Val." Sorin called. "What are you doing?"

I marched on.

Sorin caught up.

We stood, waiting for her to finish her conversation with two men dressed in tight-fitting, UPS uniforms. They fussed over her with admiring glances.

She looked over her shoulder at us. "What do you want?"

"To talk."

"We'll catch you later, girl. We're hitting the dance floor," one of the UPS guys said.

"You're our favorite queen here," the other said over his shoulder, as he sashayed toward dance floor. "Ciao."

"Thanks, Sorin. Sissy." Thomasina grunted, "I was having fun. Now what is so urgent."

"Thomasina," I said calmly. "Alberto knows you stole my idea. On Monday, he's announcing that I am the real—"

"Val, please. You exhaust me. I really don't care anymore. Let Alberto believe it was your idea."

"Hey. Don't talk to my wife that way. She's given you everything. You don't appreciate anything, do you? Val may have patience, but I don't."

"I don't care, Sorin. I don't have patience for you."

"Thomasina. Seriously. That's enough."

"Is it?" She spat. "Is it *enough* that your husband verbally abuses and breaks down your twin sister? Honestly. You're so weak. It's embarrassing. Do you know how much emotional work it took for me to get ready for this bloody ball? I did all this to support you and Dad in your carnival jobs.

"*Circus*," Sorin said. "Not carnival."

"Whatever. Just remember, Val, I sold everything and flew from England to find you."

Sorin stepped forward, inches from Thomasina. "*And* to claim two million dollars."

Thomasina took two steps back. "You are intolerable." She waved her scepter. "You have always accused me of being a hustler. You project *your* guilt on me for your taking advantage of my sister. You married my sister for her money. What's the idiom? A spade calling a spade?" She held her scepter close to her bosom. "Oh, and Val? Your Alberto's no better. He's obviously a big-time swindler. He's counting on your fortune, *our* fortune, in the years to come. He tried to get money from me."

"I don't believe it. You would've said something earlier."

"Well, he hasn't yet, but I'm sure he will. It's in his aura."

"That's ridiculous. Auras show energy. They can't predict the future."

"Sorry, Val. I love you, but you're naïve. You've made poor choices in your past, like marrying Sorin, signing a contract with Alberto, opening up to Grandmum."

Maybe she was beyond help. "No, Thomasina. I'm sorry. I love you, but you're delusional, and I'm not your therapist. You need psychological help."

"Rubbish. Stick to the facts. Where's our so-called loving Grandmum?" She spoke using her scepter. "Here we are. Both of us. Together for the first time since she let our grandfather rip us away from our mother's arms. If she'd spoken up to him, we would've grown together with our mum and been rich our whole lives. But she didn't. I don't care how old she is. Grandmum's a fraud. She should be here with—"

Sorin lunged toward her. "You're the fraud."

Thank you, my champion.

He held his ground. "Look at you. You're dressed like a frosted birthday cake, but you open your mouth, and worms crawl out."

"Terrific." Thomasina dropped her scepter to her side. "Now look who I have to deal with. Clown Judas. World famous, daredevil comic. Sis-boom-bah. He claims to be a Christian, but he lied and betrayed me."

"Hi, everyone." Romeo joined us.

"Hi Romeo," I said, quietly.

Sorin nodded.

Romeo removed his horn-rimmed glasses. "Thomasina, you look gorgeous." He opened his arms, stepping in to hug her.

"No, Romeo." She stopped him, using her scepter in a baton block. "You should go. Valthea's having a meltdown. Family stuff. *Cheerio.*"

"Whoa. Are you acting the role of your costume, or are you serious? I can't tell."

"She's serious." Sorin elbowed him. "Seriously mental."

"See, Romeo? This is what they put me through." Thomasina pressed one hand to her heart. "It doesn't matter that I'm the most beautiful girl at the ball, with the best costume money can buy, and the patience of a saint. These people won't stop attacking me."

Romeo shook his head. "I don't know why you're acting this way. Something isn't right. I'll leave you with your family. *Cheerio*, Miss Stratham." Romeo waved as he walked away. "I'll pray for you."

"Don't bother," Thomasina yelled to his back.

"Champagne, anyone?" A strolling waiter presented his tray filled with flutes of champagne.

"No, thank you," Sorin and I said.

Thomasina took a glass. "I'd love some." She took a sip. "I forgot I was at a party with you two draining me."

The waiter backed up and then hurried away.

Sorin whispered, "Men's room. I'll be back."

Thomasina hooked her scepter on the belt of her skirt. "Why does my phone keep vibrating?" She pulled her cell phone from her red-and-black, velvet wristlet. "Three missed calls. Honestly. I need to make a call."

"I'll wait here for Sorin."

Thomasina headed toward the nearby Romantic Garden area.

I had to listen in. I wove through the guests on the dance floor and then I hid in the dark space behind the Romantic Garden's middle cottage, sandwiched in by the fir trees. I placed my fingertips on the plywood, raised up on my tiptoes, and peered through a split in one of the slats.

Thomasina sat on the loveseat in front of the center cottage. Her phone rang. "Honestly." She set her champagne on one of the three stumps. "Hello? Yes, this is Haley Stevens."

Haley Stevens?

"Yes. I still need the taxi at three-fifteen, tomorrow afternoon. Please remind the driver that I've five pieces of luggage. Thank you."

She's leaving? Why is she pretending to be someone else?

Her phone rang again. She gulped some champagne before answering. "This is Haley. Relax. My phone lit up, *unknown*. I thought you were an acting agency. I do need another gig, you know. This job's done, and four-thousand only goes so far in London. The money better be in my account Monday morning. Yes. The transfer went through this afternoon. You have what you wanted. Her two and a half million."

Who was Thomasina talking to? And why did she pretend to be—

"That's why you hired me. I'm a great actress who plays a drama queen perfectly."

Actress? Was she really a girl named Haley? Pretending to be—if so, I'd strangle her. I ignored my calf cramp and listened.

"I'm at the ball. I couldn't waste the gown you had made for me. . . Why not? I'm celebrating with champagne and getting lots of attention . . . Yes. It was ridiculously easy. Apparently, no one told Valthea the family details . . . Don't worry about that. I'm a professional actress. I played things out as I saw fit . . . No. Do you believe it? They never checked on the certificate or the blood test . . . Please. Who are you to judge? You're a criminal just like the forgers . . . I know, but I'm walking away from this scheme free and clear. Who knows what you'll do next." She straightened her crown.

I was a fool. A gullible fool.

"Are you joshing? Of course, I stirred things up. Just as you asked. Here's what's amusing. These people were blooming stuck before I interfered with their lives. They've all grown . . . Too bad. I feel kind of good about that part . . . Yes. Back in London tomorrow night. Just need to tell Valthea one thing . . . Nothing related to us. Something I saw about her on a Kirlian photo . . . That camera is *not* hocus-pocus. It captures energy. Aura's are real."

What did she see? Didn't matter. I was more furious than curious.

"Don't be paranoid. Remember, Szusanna, the adoption records were sealed before baby Thomasina died on the flight."

Szusanna? The baby died? I'd never meet my — I'm going to kill this — ow. Cramp. "*Schist.*" I lost my balance and fell forward. The trees tipped over. The top of the cottage landed on the loveseat and Thomasi — Haley. I landed on the cottage.

"Get this stuff off me!" Her crown toppled, pulling her wig with it.

The photographer showed up before help came.

"Stop taking pictures," Haley shouted, reaching for her wig.

I unsnagged my costume from the cottage and helped a man lift the cottage off Haley.

"Honestly, Valthea." She pulled on her wig. "You've some serious issues. You just had to find a way to upstage me." She yanked her hem from the edge of one of the fake trees, ripping it further. "I can't take your jealousy anymore. I'm leaving to-morrow. Don't try to stop me."

A dozen or so people had gathered around us.

I spotted her cell phone on the cement floor, inches from the area's carpet. The shattered screen resembled a web. I walked up to it and lifted my foot.

"*What* is your problem?" she said, loud enough for those around to hear.

I stomped on her phone and then folded my arms in front of my chest. "*Haley.*"

Her face paled. "You know my —"

"I don't have a problem. You do. What I have is a lawyer."

Sorin and some crew guys ran up to us. One guy checked on Haley. Others moved the fallen set pieces out of the way.

Sorin rushed over to me. "Val, what's going on? Are you okay?"

"Physically, I'm fine."

"What happened?"

"Long story. Please. Just take me home."

Haley rubbed her head. "Val. It was a job. It wasn't personal. Don't hate me. Hate your aunt."

"How can I hate you? I don't know you. You're nothing to me."

Eighteen

I lay in bed, staring at the ceiling. Drowsy-eyed sheep in a moonlit pasture were nowhere to be found. Instead, relay teams of spotted cheetahs raced with my thoughts in the open savannah of my mind. I should've insisted Haley take a blood test in my presence. Why'd I let my guard down? Where did my conniving Aunt Szusanna find Haley, anyway? I should've just asked about the Kirlian camera instead of waiting for a vision. Who was this Haley girl? A phenomenal actress without a human heart, or an okay actress with borderline disorder? I fluffed my pillow and lay on my side. How would I tell my grandmother that her granddaughter, Thomasina wouldn't be visiting her any time soon—because she'd been dead for almost nineteen years?

Forty minutes after I'd fallen asleep, my alarm went off. I brushed my teeth, showered, and slipped into a black sweat suit.

"Pumpkin spice coffee?" Sorin walked into the master bath.

I put down my hairbrush and took the mug. "Thank you." I kissed him. "Don't know what I'd do without you."

"I'm worried about you. You didn't get much sleep."

"Coffee will help." I took several gulps. "I still don't want to discuss any of last night. Not until after my dress rehearsal's over."

"Got it. Totally understandable. I'm here for you. I've classes, but text if you need me. Do you want me to call Dad and your grandmother and tell them everything?"

"Dad, yes. Grama, no. I'll call her after rehearsal." I drank the rest of my coffee.

"You finished your coffee already? Better eat something." He kissed me goodbye. "Your gym bag is by the door, along with a cooler of water and fruit."

"Thanks for doing all that." I brushed my hair into a ponytail.

"Sure. Val?"

"Yeah?"

"Sorry you never got to meet your sister."

I nodded.

Sorin closed the door behind him.

I fell to my knees and sobbed. After several minutes, I prayed. Please God. Help me perform today. I don't know how I'm going to do it. I feel broken.

I parked on the mowed field behind Cirque du Palm's red-and-white stripe, big top tent. The tent, trucks, trailers, and RV's occupied the space of about two acres. I tossed my gym bag in the trailer I shared with another girl. My leotard costume and entrance cape hung in the closet. I'd change during intermission. I jogged the twenty feet to the tent, inhaling the scent of fresh-cut grass and the nearby dressage horses. I entered through a back tent flap and walked into my childhood dream world. Circus.

The back part of the tent provided nooks of space for prop boxes, a rolling rack for quick changes, and a stationary pull-up bar and gym mat for warming up.

"*Buongiorno.*" One of the four brothers of the Italian, hand-balancing act pressed into a one-armed handstand while he greeted me.

"*Buongiorno.* Morning." Focusing on my circus family freed my mind from thoughts of a fake family member.

One of the other Italian brothers warmed up on the high bar. He executed slow and controlled leg lifts. All four brothers were suave, tan, and ripped. They once performed for the pope.

The girl from the Hula-Hoop act pranced by me, talking on her cell phone in rapid-fire Russian.

The husband and wife roller skaters passed me on the other side, arguing in their thick British accents.

A thirtysomething, blonde from Paris stretched out on a portable ballet barre. Her act was in the second half of the show. She walked the high wire in ballet toe shoes.

I slipped through the split in the red theatre curtains leading to the ring. A scattering of about forty family members and friends sat in the stadium seats. Alberto and the stage manager sat in the first row discussing something.

"Another." The soundman's voice cracked over the speakers. "Another sound check, please."

The ringmaster stood left of ring, exuding bravado and tradition in his silver sequin, tuxedo jacket. He held his top hat in one hand, his mic in the other. "Testing. One tamale, two tamales. Test—"

A loud buzz pierced my ears and then stopped.

"Sorry. Again, please."

"Testing, one, two. Welcome."

I checked my rope, my rings, and the tape wrapped around them, and my cable. All good.

"Places, everyone," the stage manager yelled. "Let's go."

Artists in the first half of the show took their places. My act was second after intermission. I sat on a seat far stage left to watch the first half. I waved at Dad, sitting in the light and sound booth at the top of the stadium seats. He didn't see me. Good thing. He'd detect my lackluster energy. I felt like going home, crawling into bed, and pulling the covers over my head. Maybe I was done with this whole circus thing. I'd lived my dream. Maybe I finished all God planned for me here.

The classic circus drumroll boomed through the tent. Spotlights shined from one side of the ring to the other. The ringmaster dashed into the center. My pulse didn't race. I didn't grin ear-to-ear with excitement. I wasn't sitting at the edge of my seat. None of it.

Romeo opened with his birthday cake act, followed by the equestrian lady with her eleven dressage horses. Next came the speed juggler, with multiple listings in The Guinness Book of World Records, and then the hand balancing brothers. The roller skaters performed as if they were in-love. Romeo finished the first half with his bungee cord act. The first forty-minutes of the show hit a few glitches, but all issues were fixable, unlike my personal ones.

Intermission. I put on my costume and re-sprayed my hair with a freeze and shine product and then headed to the tent's backstage area. I lay my phone and cape on the mat and slid into a forward split. A couple of stretches later, my phone vibrated. "Hi, Grama."

"Hello, Miss Valthea. It's me. Mr. Emil."

"Hi, Mr. Emil. Before I forget, I tracked the box of Mom's journals you sent. It should've arrived at Dad's or my condo this morning. I can't wait to read them. Is Grama there, too?"

"Miss Valthea, I'm afraid I have some sad news."

"Sad news?" Did Mr. Emil know what Aunt Szusanna did? Was their more to the story? "What is it?"

"It's your grandmother. I'm afraid she's no longer with us."

"What?" I stared at my phone for a second. "Wait. I don't think I heard correctly."

"I'm sorry, Miss Valthea. Your grandmother passed away. Several hours ago. Peacefully."

"How?" I muttered. "We spoke yesterday."

"Your grandmother has been ill for quite a while. She wouldn't have held on as long as she did if it wasn't for her reuniting with you. And planning your wedding brought her great happiness." He sniffled. "Miss Valthea, you were the best thing to happen to her since you and your sister were born."

"I should've never left Romania."

"No, Valthea. Your grandmother was thrilled for your opportunity to work in America. She was especially happy knowing you and Thomasina were in each other's life again. The miracle brought her the closure she needed. She now rests in peace."

The stage manager walked by me. "Places in ten,"

"I'm so sorry," Mr. Emil said in a fluster. "I completely forgot today was your important rehearsal. I do apologize. I should've waited to call you."

"It's okay." Nothing was okay.

"I won't keep you any longer."

"I do have to go. Sorry. I know you and my grandmother were close. I'm here for you if you need anything or want to talk."

"Just like your mother."

"I'll call you after rehearsal."

"Goodbye, dear."

"Bye."

"Take your mark." The stage manager touched my shoulder.

I jumped.

"Sorry. Didn't mean to startle you."

"It's okay." I wiped my eyes and put on my cape.

Four crew guys finished sweeping up the confetti leftover in the ring from the quick-change artist's act.

I stood on my opening mark and then nodded to the man working my cable. He nodded back. I took a deep breath. I felt a little dizzy. I should've eaten breakfast. No problem. My routine was only three-and-a half minutes long and, well, up thirty-two feet in the air.

"Ladies and gentlemen, boys and girls, our next artist comes to us all the way from Bucharest, Romania. Please welcome, for the first time in America, *Val-theeea Do-braaa. . . .*"

Music of the Night, from *Phantom of the Opera* began. I glided into the ring, smiling with my head held high. I ignored the vice grip of sorrow piercing my heart. I stretched my arms wide and gracefully turned, showcasing the design on the back of my cape. Two costumers. Four months. Thousands of rhinestones, beads, and sequin appliques. Red, gold, black, and emerald. The tapestry of a moonlit rose garden with inter-weaving thorns and vines shimmered and shined.

The mist of ooo's and ahh's from the audience soothed my nerves.

A tuxedoed, circus-arts student helped remove my cape. He exited with it. I stepped up to my rope. I clipped the safety cable to my waistband, nodded to my crew guy, and climbed, arms only, toward my rings. The angel of music took me under her wings and my routine flowed. I wrapped one leg around the rope and stretched into a split, and held it, smiling. Performers must provide space for their audience to express their glee. I reached for my rings, and with all my strength, pulled myself up into a straight arm hold.

More applause.

I swooped around and held an inversion. I continued through backbends, splits, and full-body rotations.

Next, in daredevil fashion, I swung forward and back like a pendulum in wide arcs, thirty-five feet above the cement ring floor. I swung holding the rings, my body dangling un-derneath me. I swung standing with feet in the rings and hold-ing onto each ring's cable. I swung hanging from the back of my knees with my arms reaching to my audience. I blew them a kiss. They cheered. Rock star adrenaline whipped through my veins. I loved performing.

The ringmaster's voice bolted from the speakers. "Ladies and gentlemen."

I swung my body up to a seated position. My legs stretched through the rings. My arms around each cable line.

He continued. "I must ask for your complete silence as Miss Valthea prepares to fully release from the Roman rings, perform a full somersault, and finish holding on to a single rope. Ladies and gentlemen, Miss Valthea." He raised his top hat and backed out of the spotlight.

A drumroll boomed over the speakers. The unmistakable sound of a circus drumroll elicited the same anxious thrill in all audiences around the world, no matter their creed, gender, or country.

I smoothed my ponytail. I wiped my palms. I raised my brows, feigning nervousness and then nodded to my crew guy. All part of the act.

He nodded back and then pulled and pushed me via the rope for several seconds before releasing it.

I swung higher and fuller than before. Four, three, two … I shifted from swinging seated, to my knees, and then to my hands. I swung back and forth once more. I let go of the rings. Completed one somersault. Spotted my rope. Grabbed it and held on tight, while wrapping my legs around it.

Cymbals crashed, and the crowd cheered.

I waved and smiled. My head felt light, but my peppy exit music kept me going. I unhooked my cable, let it drop, and climbed down my rope. Abs tight. Legs straight out, perpendicular to my torso. Suddenly, the tent spun. All went black.

I opened my eyes. Alberto, our two, on-hand paramedics, and the stage manager, encircled me. I lay flat on the mat below my rings, in semi-darkness.

"Can you move your legs?" Beads of sweat formed on Alberto's forehead.

"Please, sir. Let us do our job." The first medic checked my pulse.

"Can you wiggle your toes?" the second medic asked. He didn't look old enough to shave.

"My back's fine." I held my shoulder and wiggled my toes. "It's my shoulder. I think I tore something."

The stage manager spoke into his walkie-talkie and left the ring. "Mary Had a Little Lamb" played on the speakers. It was one of our clowns' extra bits in case of a gap, or an accident.

"Thank God, you're okay." Alberto wiped his brow. "These guys are going to take care of you. Your dad's coming down from lighting."

"Thanks, Alberto. I know the show must go on."

Alberto nodded. "Your act was flawless."

"Really?"

"Absolutely. I'll check on you in a bit."

The medics helped me stand and then walked me to the far right, to seats in the first row.

"Let's check your range. Let me know when it hurts." The first medic took my right arm and barely lifted away from my side.

"Ow."

The younger medic wrapped my shoulder and then helped me put on a sling. "Is that comfortable?"

"Hey, doctor wannabes. Get her to the emergency room." Haley hurried toward us from the nearest entrance. She wore the same black jeans and sweater she had on when we first met.

"What are you doing here?" Now I felt nauseated. "Quiet down. A show's going on."

She stomped. "Are you putting Valthea on a stretcher, or do I have to do it?"

"Shhh. I can walk. It's my shoulder. Go catch your flight."

The stage manager quickly walked up to me. "Here." He handed me a juice box with a straw. He sat my handbag, slippers, and red sweat suit on the seat next to me. "Do exactly what the doc tells you. You were fantastic today. We want you back as soon as possible."

"Thanks." I sipped some juice and carefully pulled on my sweat pants.

Haley whispered, "I need to tell you a couple important things before I go."

"Val." Dad ran up to me. "You okay? What hurts? Did you faint? How's your back?"

192

"Back's fine. It's my shoulder. Feels like I pulled something." I fought back the tears. "How long's this going to take to heal? I just got here. I can't—"

"We'll figure it out." He brushed a few stray hairs from my face. "First we need to—"

"Get her to a hospital." Haley nudged one of the paramedics.

"Why are you here? How dare you show your face after what you put my daughter through? Just go."

"I will as soon as Valthea's with a doctor. And after I talk to her."

The younger medic whispered, "Do you want to go to the emergency room?"

"No. I fainted and fell five or six feet onto a mat. No big deal."

Haley looked me dead in the eye. "It is a big deal when you're pregnant."

"You're pregnant? Get the stretcher." Dad shouted. "Why didn't tell me?"

"I didn't know, er, I'm not. I don't think."

"Is it possible you're pregnant?" the older medic asked.

"It is possible."

"I'll get the wheelchair from the truck."

The young medic closed his kit. "We're taking you to the ER."

"Okay." I didn't want to see or talk to Haley. But— "Why do you say I'm pregnant?"

"Your aura."

"Enough of your stories." Dad flicked his hand in dismissal.

"Mr. Dobra, I'm sorry," she said, quietly. "It's true. I lied to you and your family. But auras don't lie."

"It's all absurd." Dad huffed.

"That's one reason I stopped here on my way to the airport. To tell Valthea."

The medic returned with the wheelchair.

Dad turned his back to Haley. "I have to finish the show. Text me with the hospital's address and when you've more information." He kissed me and then ran up the stairs and back into the light booth.

The medics wheeled me out the tent and toward their nearby ambulance truck.

Haley followed. "I know you hate me. You don't have to believe me. I don't see auras. I use a — "

"Special camera. I know. Just tell me what you saw." I held my flat belly.

"Kirlian camera photographs show lights and colors around a living thing. All living things. I hadn't noticed it until this morning, packing my stuff. Your most recent photo. Swipes of orange and silver light."

"Which means what?"

"A baby."

Nineteen

I texted Sorin on the way to the emergency room. Told him everything, although he wouldn't see the message until after his lab class.

Haley insisted on coming to the hospital. She had something to tell me, besides her seeing orange and silver in my photograph. She followed the ambulance truck and now waited with me in the reception area. She sat across from me in a separate row of chairs. Smart to give me space.

"Haley." I held up the clipboard the receptionist gave me. "I can't talk or listen yet."

She nodded. "I understand. I'll be right back."

Thirty minutes later, I'd filled out the pastel medical forms, handed over my passport and insurance card for photocopying, and peed into a cup. A nurse would check it with a pregnancy stick test in another room. I waited in the reception area.

"Here." Haley handed me a bottled water and a granola bar. She sat in her same chair.

"Thanks. I am hungry."

After a few minutes, a different nurse came by to confirm I'd no broken bones sticking out of my body.

"Nothing's broken." I moved my arm slowly in the direction that didn't hurt. "I've a bad tear of some kind. I know because I'm an athlete. A circus performer."

She smiled. "Costume gave you away." unrolled a new arm sling. "This will keep you comfortable." She put it on me and then re-draped my sweat jacket over my shoulders. "I've seen many circus performers over the years. Tough breed. Amazing healers."

I sat straighter, proud to part of such a breed.

"It'll be thrity to forty minutes before a doctor will see you." She smiled at Haley. "Least you have your sister to keep you company."

195

"Oh, she's not my —"

Another nurse called her. She hurried down the hall.

I tore off the wrapper of the granola bar. "Okay, Haley. Say what you need to say." I bit into the bar.

"All right." She sat forward on her chair. "I came to your rehearsal to tell you of your pregnancy and —"

"*Possible* pregnancy."

She nodded.

"By the way, not that you care but, last night my Grama Alessia died."

"Oh no."

"Your *boss* probably already told you."

"No, she didn't. And she isn't my boss. I'm sorry, Valthea. I know you two were close."

"Babe!" Sorin rushed toward me from the elevator. He hugged me, careful to avoid my shoulder. "Got here as soon as I could. How are you? How's your shoulder?"

"Everything's better now that you're here."

"Is it true?" He stood proud as an expectant alpha wolf. "We're going to have a baby?"

"Don't know yet. It's possible. Missed my last period. But that could be because of training, or the stress from moving, or anything. We'll find out. Uh, Sorin. Haley's behind you."

"What?" He whipped around. "What are you doing here? Get out of our life already."

"Sorin. Wait. Haley brought me here. And she needs to tell me something. She's waited an hour."

"I don't care if she's waited a hundred hours." He pointed. "There's the elevator, Haley. Go and never come back."

"Haley, give us a few minutes."

"Val."

"Sorin. I want to hear what she has to say."

"I'll take a walk." Haley scooted out of the waiting area.

"You must've hit your head." He sat next to me. "Why do you want to hear more lies from that girl? You've given her more than enough of your time and life. Our time and our life. Tell her to go home."

"I will. After I hear what she has to say."

"I'm just trying to protect my family."

I rested my head on his shoulder. *Family*. I loved the very word.

One of the receptionists walked up to us. "Doctor Zhao will see you shortly. It's a quiet ER day. Here you go." She handed me my passport and insurance card. "All set."

I tucked them into the side, zip up pocket in my purse.

"Val!" Dad and Romeo Bach shot past a couple of people exiting the elevator. They blasted into the waiting area. "My precious daughter, are you all right? Am I going to be a grandfather? Is the baby okay? What did the doctor say about your shoulder? Did the fall hurt the baby?"

"Sheesh, Dad. Ease up. Val's been through a tornado over the last twenty-four hours."

"I don't know anything yet. I haven't seen a doctor."

Dad kissed me on my cheek and then sat in the chair on the other side of me. "Isn't this great? A baby in America. What a blessing."

"Dad. Stop. She's doesn't know yet."

Romeo sat on one of the chairs across from us. "How's your shoulder feel?"

"I won't be flying through the air any time soon. What will Alberto do about my act?"

Romeo shrugged. "Injuries are part of circus. Be grateful it was only five-feet. You'll heal. Alberto will *fill* your spot. But you can teach, coach, and work on the student show."

"That's all fantastic. But I'm anxious to perform in America. It's been a dream of mine since I was a kid."

"You will. Heal and train. Heal and train. Right, doc?"

"I'm not a doctor yet. But yeah." Sorin nodded. "Romeo's right."

"Absolutely." Dad punched a fist in the air. "Your shoulder will heal. You'll perform. And then, you'll have the baby. I can't wait."

"Dad. You're not helping."

"I appreciate everyone's positivity. But I can face facts. Everything's gone wrong. I prayed to work in America and expand my family. I thought God answered my prayers when I signed on as a solo in an American circus and met my long-lost twin sister. Looks like both have been taken away from me."

"Nothing was taken from you," Romeo said quietly. "We all have free will. You chose a high-risk field. Your aunt and Haley made greedy choices. They acted on them. You believed everything Thomasina-Haley said. You didn't wait for her to earn your trust. I know, because I did the same thing."

Sorin kissed my cheek. "Babe, this is a temporary low. A high's around the corner for you. I'm sure of it."

"Until then, you have all of us. Ha!" Dad slapped one thigh. "What more could you want?"

Romeo patted Dad on the back. "You're surrounded by family and friends. Your shoulder will heal. You're sitting *out* one circus season, not sitting *in* a wheelchair for the rest of your life."

"I've much to be grateful for."

Haley slipped back into the waiting area.

Dad took a double take. "You?"

"Haley, thank you for insisting my wife see a doctor, but you can go." Sorin kept my hand in his. "Her real family is here now."

"Yeah." Dad glanced at the wall clock. "Doesn't your flight leaves in a couple hours?"

"Better hurry and get your paycheck from Szusanna before she realizes our lawyer is coming after her. I'm sure she paid you enough to get your life going. Plus, you banked that two-thousand my wife gave you to hold you over." Sorin half-saluted. "Cheerio, Haley."

"Valthea," Haley whispered. "I'll go, but I need to tell you—"

"She doesn't want to hear it," Dad yelled. "You've put her though enough. Now she can't perform for months."

"Dad. Sorin. Haley didn't make me fall. I fainted. I didn't eat this morning. The fall is my fault."

Sorin shook his head.

Dad looked away.

Haley and Romeo locked eyes.

I cupped the elbow of my injured arm, alleviating some of the pain in my shoulder. "Go ahead, Haley. I'm listening."

She broke from Romeo's stare. "Okay. This morning, when I was packing my suitcases, a delivery guy knocked on the door. He needed a signature for a heavy box sent from Romania. The box was crushed and ripped partway open. I didn't want to sign for it if the contents were destroyed, so I opened it in front of him. Inside was a black case with four diaries."

"Finally." I hopped out of my chair. Feeling light-headed, I sat back down.

"What diaries?" Sorin asked.

"My mother's journals. I told you about them. I'm so excited."

"Hold on." Sorin held up one hand in stop position. "Haley. It's against the law to open other people's mail."

I lowered his arm. "Did you leave the box in my dad's condo?"

"Yes" She shifted in her chair. I threw out the cardboard box, took the journals out of the black case, and laid them on your dad's coffee table."

"Okay. Good."

"Val, I couldn't help myself. I skimmed through the diaries. Thought I'd read just a little. But then . . . I read a lot."

"What?"

"Sacrilege!" Dad restrained his inner panther by clawing the arms of his chair. "You don't deserve to touch the same piece of paper my Gisella touched, never mind read her personal diary."

"You read my mother's journals? Before me?"

"Not all of them. I didn't finish the last one. But it's good I read them. I learned the truth."

"What truth?" Dad balled his claws into fists.

"Gisella Adamescu wrote about everything and everyone. She wrote about her father, her mum, and Szusanna. She also wrote a lot about you, Mr. Dobra."

"They weren't yours to read." I wanted to choke her. "You're as irreverent as the fake Thomasina."

Sorin put his arm around me. "Haley. It's time for you to go."

"I will. I'm sorry. But I discovered —"

"No." Dad stood. His black Gypsy boots firmly planted. His arms folded across his chest "It was wrong of you. Period."

"Excuse me, everyone." Romeo moved his chair in closer to us. "I'm not family, but Haley will be gone soon. Forever. It might be wise to hear what she has to say."

Haley spent weeks spinning me, Sorin, and dad into her web of lies and manipulation. She did the same to Romeo Bach. If Romeo managed patience after experiencing her sticky poison, I could listen to her for five more minutes.

"You're right, Romeo. Haley, you have five-minutes." I folded my hands on my lap.

"Okay. First, Sorin, Mr. Dobra. I apologize for meddling in your lives. Whether I was hired to do so, or not, you are good people. You didn't deserve what I put you through. Romeo, I'm sorry for —"

"Don't worry about me." Romeo tipped his head my way. "It's Valthea who deserves your attention."

"Right. Valthea. I'm sorry. I now know everything Szusanna told me was a lie. Truths completely twisted around. Although, I'd been a complete jerk and meanie the whole time, you kept believing in me. You gave me oodles of chances to redeem myself. Who would do that? Only a kind person, like you, or your mother, or . . .*my* mother."

For once, I believed her.

"I know you thought we were sisters, but even if we were, you went bonkers beyond your sisterly duty. The *Thomasina* you met didn't deserve your patience or your unconditional love."

"Neither does *Haley*." Sorin held my hand.

My champion. "For the record, it wasn't patience, but naiveté. I didn't do my due diligence on you."

"Bottom line—you don't deserve my wife's forgiveness. I don't care if you were brainwashed. Come on. A seven-year-old knows the difference between right and wrong. And what you did was clearly wrong."

"I accept that. I justified my choices as revenge.

"Revenge for what?" Dad paced in front of us. "My daughter never did anything to you."

"The revenge was against my own whacked out family. Val, after reading your mum's diaries, I realized Szusanna had flipped the truth about her and her sister."

"What do you mean?" I walked to the nearby waste basket and threw away the remains of my granola bar. I was so done with Haley.

"Szusanna painted herself the angel and victim. She painted Gisella the evil, conniving bully."

"That woman. She's still the same." Dad continued to pace. "After all these years."

"Your Aunt Szusanna brainwashed me into thinking that it was your mum who robbed her of their parents' attention, her inheritance, and even you, Mr. Dobra. Back when you were teens."

"Malevolent witch."

"Dad. Please. Sit."

"Val." Dad sat on the edge of his seat. "From the moment I saw Szusanna, I knew she was trouble. It didn't matter that Gisella held my entire attention and my whole heart. She— never mind." He leaned back in his chair. "Finish your story, Haley."

She nodded. "Val, when Szusanna hired me, she went on and on about how you were your mum's evil spawn. She said you never visited her or your grandmother until you turned eighteen, and then, only because you expected to receive a trust fund."

"Idiotic." Dad stood. "My daughter didn't know she had an aunt and a grandmother until she was eighteen. Pack of lies. All of it. I could just kill that orange-haired—"

"Easy, Dad. She's not worth it." Sorin handed me my water bottle.

"Haley, give us an example of Szusanna's flipping stories." I finished my water, hoping hydration helped my brain wrap around Haley's findings.

"It wasn't Szusanna who her father, and the household staff, referred to as an angel. It was Gisella."

"Everyone knew that," Dad grumbled. "That doesn't count."

"Szusanna also told me Gisella started smoking cigarettes at fourteen. But as you know, Szusanna's the longtime smoker. She has the skin and voice to prove it."

Dad wagged his finger. "Gisella never smoked.

Haley nodded. "I was also told that Gisella jabbed lit cigarettes into Szusanna's thighs and arms and then laughed at her when she jumped and pulled away."

I shuddered. I wished I were there to defend my mother.

"This too, was a lie. Gisella wrote over and over about Szusanna burning her." Haley took a breath. "I know what those burns feel like. My father used to do that to me when I fell asleep on the couch. He thought it was funny."

Romeo walked over and sat on the arm of Haley's chair. She looked up and smiled at him.

"Continue," Sorin said.

"It was sad. Reading the diaries. Most nights, Gisella cried herself to sleep wondering why her sister hated her so much."

"I can't bear the thought." Dad dropped his face into his hands. "My poor Gisella. I didn't know. I saw a mark once. She said it was from candles. If only I knew." He looked up. "Why didn't she say something?"

"Because she knew if she ever told their parents, Szusanna would lie. Big time. She'd tell them that Gisella did those things to her. She'd burn herself to cover the lie and then point the finger at her sister. Val, your Grandmum descended from aristocracy, but your grandfather came from a militant lineage. Gisella would've been lashed with a belt."

"Monster," Dad mumbled.

"Gisella wrote of her weak heart and of feeling tired and sleep deprived. She knew if her father went into a rage and beat her, she may never recover."

"You mean *die*?" Sorin asked.

Sorin asked the question I could not.

"Physically, Gisella was fragile. She knew a beating from her huge, enraged father would kill her. If she died, it'd break her mother's heart and tear apart their family. She didn't want that."

I wiped my eyes on my sweat jacket sleeve.

"Your mum also wrote prayers in her diaries. Prayers of protection, guidance, and gratitude. She even wrote a prayer requesting that God have mercy on Szusanna. Do you believe that?" Haley's eyes bugged. "She was willing to forgive that sick woman."

"I believe it." Dad's eyes welled.

"Wow." Romeo shook his head.

Everything Haley shared confirmed the visions I'd seen of Aunt Szusanna when I met her, over a year ago, at my great aunt's funeral.

"Val, is this your first time hearing all this? About your aunt?" Romeo asked. "You okay?"

"I knew a lot of it, yes. Thank you."

"You couldn't have." Haley's sharp tone was all too familiar. "The diaries indicated that only your mum and Szusanna knew. How could you know?"

"Uh, I uh—"

"My wife's tired." Sorin put his arm around me. "Just finish the story. She needs to rest."

Good cover.

"I'm an actress, but not compared to your aunt. When we met, she offered me this 'reality acting job'. She then performed a monologue, complete with tears, about this next story."

Crocodile tears. "Go on."

"Your mum wrote many times about the mean things Szusanna did to her. It went on from the time she was twelve until about fifteen."

"Like what?" Sorin asked.

"At night, Szusanna would sneak into Gisella's bedroom with a pair of scissors."

I didn't want to know.

"She slashed Gisella's favorite dresses. She jabbed her sister's stuffed teddy bears and tigers until their stuffing came out and then cut off their limbs. She kidnapped Gisella's best dolls, strip them naked, and then chop off their shiny hair until only a scraggly patch or two remained. Gisella wrote of awaking to seeing her dolls tortured. She cried and prayed. Not because they were her favorite dolls. Or because her sister hurt her feelings. The post-Szusanna dolls reminded Gisella of the horrific photographs she'd seen in history class. Women, shaved, stripped, and starving in Nazi concentration camps. Many mornings, Gisella awoke to finding long strands of her own strawberry blonde hair laying on her pillow."

Romeo shook his head.

Dad buried his face in his hands.

I wanted to throw up.

"It gets worse," Haley continued. "Gisella lay awake for hours every night, afraid to fall asleep. As soon as she did, she'd wake up to Szusanna hovering over her, ccovering her mouth and burning her with a cigarette She burned Gisella arms, legs, and even her neck. Other nights, worse nights, Szusanna sat on Gisella, holding her down while stuffing a balled-up scarf into her mouth. She'd keep it there, laughing as her sister squirmed and fought to breathe. At the last possible second, Szusanna would pull the scarf from Gisella's mouth. One time, Szusanna timed it wrong, and Gisella passed out. After that, Szusanna stopped gagging her. She only burned her."

"Makes me sick." Dad wiped his eyes. "A devil child makes for an evil woman."

"I hate myself for falling for such a woman's lies. But more so, I'm sorry for my becoming part of those lies. There's no excuse. I'm one-hundred percent responsible for my actions."

"Least you admit it."

"Oh my God. You can't stop there. I need to hear about something she wrote that was happy." I rested my head on Sorin's shoulder.

Haley perked up. "Okay. In her last diary, titled New York, your mum wrote on and on about how much she loved and adored you and your twin. She found it curious how her twin babies acted so much alike, but also dramatically different. Thomasina cried a lot. You cried only when hungry. Thomasina acted finicky and fussy. You stayed pretty much cheery and even tempered."

My heart felt light for the first time in days. Was I my mother's favorite? I smiled. I didn't stop myself from wanting it to be true. My phone vibrated in my sweat pant pocket. I pulled it out. Read it through three times. "Haley. Why?" I passed my phone to Sorin. "Why'd you do it?"

"Val, I apologize. The box was half-open. The guy wanted me to sign for—"

"No, not that." I shook my head. "You were free and clear. Cash in the bank. Better life ahead."

"I don't believe it." Sorin handed me my phone.

"I just got an email from the bank. Half the inheritance, and the two-thousand-dollar deposit I made for you a week ago, is back in my checking account. Why?"

"The money doesn't belong to me. Or to Szusanna. I transferred the money from the Thomasina Stratham checking account to your checking account. The Thomasina account is now closed. Screw Szusanna. I want no part of her, her lies, or her schemes. Screw my bad choices. I signed up for counseling, back in England."

"Good," Sorin said. "You're finally doing the right thing."

"I'm trying. I'm staying with theatre friends in London until I get back on my feet. And Mr. Dobra, I left an apology letter in an envelope for Miss Colleen. She's a nice lady. I hope everything works out for you two."

Dad nodded once.

My emotions swirled together. "I'm happy about your wise decisions. Counseling's great. It'll help with closure and moving forward. But, Haley, I can't let you go home penniless."

"Babe. Let her go."

"It's okay, Valthea. Thank you. I don't want anything. Truly."

"Hello, everyone." A round man with smiling, coal-black eyes walked up to us. He wore a white lab jacket and stethoscope around his neck. "Hi Valthea. I'm Doctor Zhao. That's Zhao, like wow, but without the wow factor." He chuckled.

Dr. Zhao reminded me of a panda bear.

He approached with a light step and an air of kindness. "Valthea, I'm sorry about your fall." He tipped his head. "Is this your family?"

I touched Sorin's arm and then gestured to Dad. "This is my husband, Sorin. My dad, Cosmo, and—"

"I'm Romeo Bach. A friend."

"How wonderful to meet you all." Doctor Zhao's eyes twinkled. "And you must be Valthea's sister."

"Uh, no. I'm Haley."

"A friend," I said.

Haley smiled.

"Ah." Doctor Zhao pointed one index finger upward. "Apparently, a good friend. The medic told the receptionist that Haley insisted you see a doctor."

"Actually, my wife would've come in on her own. She didn't need—"

"No, Sorin, I probably wouldn't have come in. I'm stubborn that way."

"In any case," Dr. Zhao said, "good thing you did. You seem fine overall. But after your tumble, we need to be sure. Now, before we go into that or talk about your shoulder and therapy options, I may have some good news for you."

"She has a bun in the oven?" Haley's cheeks glowed.

"I'd like to do an ultrasound to confirm, but Valthea," Doctor Zhao smiled. "With your history of fraternal twins, you may have two buns in the oven."

"Twins?" I grabbed Sorin's arm.

Sorin hugged and kissed me.

"Two babies!" Dad punched the air. "Yes."

Romeo and Haley hesitated, but then slapped each other a high-five.

Sorin brushed my bangs to one side and whispered, "You're going to make a wonderful mother."

"Thank you." Him saying that meant the world to me.

C.K. Mallick

"Now, now." Dr. Zhao waved his folder. "We don't know about the twins conclusively."

"Excuse me, Doctor." Dad fidgeted his panther ring. "Do you know if my daughter is having boys or —"

"Girls?" Haley asked.

"Or maybe a girl and a boy?" Sorin piped in.

Doctor Zhao chuckled. "It's a little early to know gender."

"Ooo, Val. I forgot to tell you. In your mum's diaries —"

"Not now, Haley. Val will read them for herself when we get home."

Haley ignored Sorin and continued unspinning her enthusiasm. "Gisella mentioned *three* sets of fraternal twins on your mum's side. In each case, the twins were opposite in temperament and demeanor. Hopefully, you won't have another Szusanna. Can you imagine?"

My heart skipped a beat.

"I don't know about all that." Dr. Zhao glanced at his watch. "But Valthea, we can do the ultrasound now if you like."

"Absolutely. I want to."

"Excellent." Dr. Zhao tucked his folder under his arm. "You can decide who'd you'd like in the room. Be back in a couple of minutes." He toddled off to the main desk.

"Hope you guys don't mind," I said. "But I'd like it to just be Sorin and me,"

"Of course." Dad kissed us both. "It's a sacred moment. We'll wait here."

Romeo patted Sorin on the back. "What a blessing. I'll wait here with your dad."

Haley stood, her handbag on the crook of arm. "Well, Valthea. You've a great support team here. I wish you the very best. Once again, I apologize for all the trouble I stirred."

"Apology accepted. But Haley, here's what's interesting. Over the last couple of weeks, Aunt Szusanna's plot and your manipulations didn't break down my family. Instead, Dad, Sorin, and me, we're all stronger. Dad gained closure in a couple of areas of his life. He found a great woman. He's trusting his feelings. Sorin shared feelings he stuffed long ago. He also owns his choice to pursue acupuncture. Me? I accept the creativity I never knew I had. From show concepts to—"

"Babies?" She smiled.

"Yes. I've also learned about giving people second chances. Anyway, I'm proud of my family. We survived Aunt Szusanna and the fake Thomasina. It won't be the last challenge of our life, but we'll always be family. Our show will always go on."

Haley wiped the first real tear I'd seen her shed. "I wish I had a family like yours. Wish I had a sister like you."

"You did," Sorin mumbled. "And you blew it."

"You're right. I did blow it. But I'm not going to blow any more of my life. Well, time for me to go. Plane to catch. Goodbye everyone." She headed toward the elevator but then turned. "Oh, and Val. Forget all those stories and superstitious rhymes about twins. One good. One evil."

"I already have." I smiled, softly rubbing my flat tummy. "Both my babies will turn out sunshine yellow."

Haley stepped into the elevator. "I'm sure they will." She smiled and waved. Her spider necklace twinkled.

Acknowledgments:

Thank you to the spectacular circus artists whom I had the privilege of interviewing:

Bello Nock, 7th generation circus family, world famous, daredevil clown, appeared on *America's Got Talent*, featured in the *Guinness Book of World Records*.

Blake Wallenda, 7th generation circus, world famous Wallenda family, daredevil, wire walker, exotic animal trainer, acrobat, freelance circus performer

Khera Lorraine Smith, Sailor Circus graduate, aerialist and wire walker, performed with Big Apple Circus, Circus Sarasota

Thank you to all involved with the **Circus Arts Conservatory** for their support on my book series journey. Special thanks to: **Mary Jo Heider, Jennifer Mitchell, Pedro Reis**.

Thank you to those who edited, read through, or sponsored **Thomasina: The Twin**:

Kim Hackett, Kathy Needham, Annette Masters, editor, **Patricia Sofia, Scott Zeus Smith**, sponsorship.

Special thanks to: **Michelle Brault, Jeff Hoffman, Jo Mallick, Marie Rizzuti, Angel Shutt, Natalie Sivetz, Mirjana Spurnic**

Thank you to my patient and encouraging publisher, **Wendy Dingwall**, publisher, novelist

Thanks to **Tracy Arendt** for her collaborative and final art on The Twin's book cover

Thank you to my other family, friends, and co-workers who endured my reading bits to them and asking them random questions!

Book 3

DASHA: CHAIN BREAKER

My sister is a cult leader. Danica walks the dark side. She denies it, but I know it's true. Can't fool your fraternal twin. Some teens deal with academic, social media, and family pressure via bullying, cutting, or taking drugs. I walk high-wire. Danica collects people. She usurps the rejected and desperate wannabes of our high school. She welcomes them into her ever-increasing pack of pawns she calls, *The Family*. She is a self-proclaimed influencer. *They* are like dazed social media followers, likers, and fans come alive.

My name is Dasha. I've two best friends. I study the circus arts, and high-wire's my favorite. Far from earth. Closer to heaven. Growing up, I've dealt with, and managed to subdue, pretty much all my sister's conniving plots and diabolical games. But what about this newest one? It's the sickest, grand scheme she's ever concocted. Or should I say, *copied*. Cyanide Kool-Aid. Group suicide. She wouldn't see it through. Or would she? I'm a student circus performer. *Not* a cult-interventionist *or* demonic stronghold intercessor. Blasted Danica. I wanted to banish her from the planet. But first, I need to save her and her gang. I kissed my cross pendant. God be with me.

ABOUT THE AUTHOR

C.K.'s eclectic past and present greatly affects her fiction and non-fiction writing. She's worked over twenty years in the dance/entertainment field and in the cosmetics industry. Her volunteer work includes stints at a V.A. hospital, The Big Cat Rescue, The Boys & Girls Club, Circus Arts Conservatory and Bayside Community Church.

The initial sparks of inspiration for *Valthea: I Read People* came from two of C.K.'s childhood memories. She grew up near Venice, Florida, the former winter home of Ringling Brothers and Barnum and Bailey Circus, and she loved listening to stories of the "intuitive" great-grandmother she never met. Thirty years later, C.K.'s story ideas rekindled after watching a performance of Circus Sarasota featuring the legendary and beautiful aerialist, Dolly Jacobs-Reis and the world-famous daredevil clown, Bello Nock, and other circus artists. She wrote *Valthea: I Read People* and *Thomasina: The Twin* while interviewing performers, crew, and coaches.

C. K. relishes her time spent with the woodlands and beaches of her home city of Sarasota, Florida. She keeps her energy high and her mind inspired by maintaining a healthy lifestyle and listening to people's stories. She considers herself blessed, knowing her books come into the homes and hands of so many women, men and children of all ages!

Other Books by the Author:
Valthea: I Read People; The Daughters, Book One

Short Stories:
Skate Walker, Hooked on Hockey-Chicken Soup for the Soul
Face Time, Let's Talk: Anthology collection
Places Everyone! The Florida Writer magazine.